He Will Never Know

Books by Toney Larson

Young Adult

<u>Legends of Draven Series</u>

Book One: Growing Amaranth
Book Two: Unmasking Cassandra
Book Three: Engaging Helen
Cornelius Wilbur's Book of Astounding and Magnificent Riddles

Coming Soon

Book Four: Pursuing Hannah
Book Five: Daring Hazel

Adult Non-Fiction

Surviving the Moment:
Powering Through Negative Thinking

TONEY LARSON

He Will Never Know

Tall Tower
Publishing

Text copyright 2021 by Toney Larson. All rights reserved.

Interior Design by Octavo Book Covers.

Cover design by The Red Leaf Book Design /
www.redleafbookdesign.com.

No part of this publication may be reproduced, or stored in a retrieval system, or transmitted in any form or by any means electronic, mechanical, photocopying, recording, or otherwise without the express, written consent of the author.

For information regarding permissions, email to:
Talltowerpublishing@gmail.com
Attention Of: Permissions Department

ISBN-13: 978-0-9903576-5-0
Library of Congress Control Number: 2022901650

Printed in the United States of America.
First Edition.

Tall Tower Publishing

To my secret lover

Table of Contents

Chapter 1 1
Chapter 2 8
Chapter 3 14
Chapter 4 19
Chapter 5 32
Chapter 6 42
Chapter 7 47
Chapter 8 55
Chapter 9 61
Chapter 10 66
Chapter 11 75
Chapter 12 81
Chapter 13 86
Chapter 14 90
Chapter 15 95
Chapter 16 100
Chapter 17 110
Chapter 18 116
Chapter 19 121
Chapter 20 128
Chapter 21 135
Chapter 22 140
Chapter 23 143
Chapter 24 154
Epilogue 160

Chapter 1

Annie Allred gripped the oars, her muscles tensing as the rain came down in the dark, cloud filled night. The boat swayed from side to side, threatening to knock her into the water, along with the few possessions she had thrown in a sack. If she traversed the river, she would make it across to her hometown, and she would find him. Annie had no idea where he was or what he was doing, but she would get to him.

As she gave a mighty pull on the oars, sure she could make it across within minutes, she heard screaming behind her. She spun around, suddenly standing on dry ground in front of a security guard, his face furiously red. She had already been warned once not to cross the river. Now she was under arrest.

Within a blink, she was handcuffed and thrown into an odd sort of housing jail. It was decently furnished and had three rooms, not like any jail she had ever seen. It was comfortable, but she couldn't stay there. She had to find him. She twisted the handcuffs they had left on, as they deemed her too dangerous. She had just managed to slide her small hand out of one of them when someone came to the door.

She was prepared to make a mad fight to escape, but when the door opened, she sank to her knees as *he* walked into the room. He grabbed her, kneeling in front of her, desperately explaining that he had heard she was there, had talked his way into the jail, and now that he had her, he would never leave her again. He took her in his arms, and she cried, telling him how hard she had tried to find him. He said he knew as he leaned down, his face so close to her…

Then she collapsed in a bout of pain.

Annie opened her eyes. She was not in a fancy jailhouse, which had been far nicer than her own apartment. The brick wall of her studio stared back at her, rusty red and bare. Her sheets were crumpled on the floor and her blanket was hanging on one foot, as if refusing to die like this. She shook it off. The pain that woke her resonated through her abdomen, and she took a breath. Of *course* cramps would wake her from the most romantic dream she'd had in years.

She rolled out of bed, landing on the floor in a heap, joining her blanket to mope on the floor. Perhaps if she fell back asleep, the dream would pick up where it left off.

Another round of cramps hit, and she dragged herself off the floor for a glass of water, ibuprofen, and a heating pad. She dropped onto her worn-out love seat at the foot of the bed, one of the few pieces of furniture in the room and the only that had survived the cut. The divorce had left her pocketbook full, but her furnishings sparse.

As far as divorces go, this one was straightforward. Charles had fallen in love with Melissa, had an affair, and felt so guilty that everything was evenly split—sold off, then evenly split. The kids, their two girls, had taken the divorce as well as any children, declaring they would never forgive their father and choosing to live with their mother. With the house sold, the girls' room was packed up and currently filling the corner of their studio apartment. The kids were sent off to their grandmother for the summer while Annie sorted out finding a new house and getting herself together, since she was, understandably, a mess. It wasn't even June yet.

Melissa, Annie bitterly had to concede, was actually a very nice person. She was smart, kind—even to the ex-wife—and her children liked her, though they pretended they didn't out of anger at their father. Melissa had worked at the same office as Annie's husband, and they were constantly thrown together on projects. It was almost inevitable that feelings would arise.

This was where Annie secretly took a little of the blame—though she never admitted that out loud—by being an independent author. Being an author wasn't the problem; being such a devoted, hardcore workaholic of an author was the problem. While the kids were in school, she was typing at the kitchen table. While her family ate dinner, she was typing in the bedroom. When her husband had come to confess his infidelity, it took him three days to talk to her because she was too busy typing to listen.

In her defense, she was a prolific writer with a large number of books that had supplemented their income very well. However, it had also reduced her marriage to one of convenience and, frankly, irritation. She hadn't liked being bothered. But she wasn't an unreasonable person. The moment she realized her marriage was in jeopardy, she had wizened up, and was willing to ignore his mistake and seek counseling, go on dates, fall in love again. But he was beyond all that. Melissa got off work at the same time he did. Melissa spent all day flirting with him. Melissa was the new love of his life. Life was too short to spend it in a counselor's office, hoping something would change. So he left with Melissa—becoming the guilty party—and abandoned his preoccupied wife.

Through their mutual and amicable agreement of separation and parenting plan, the divorce was finalized fairly quickly, and the wedding followed shortly after. She had to give her ex-husband some credit. He was honorable, at least. Sure, he was a cheating, rotten, despicable dirt bag, but he wasn't a scoundrel. This wasn't a midlife fling, but a genuine relationship with an actual person, which was more than she could say about her affair with her laptop, where the relationships only existed in her mind. Now she sat in her temporary apartment surrounded by boxes belonging to her children, wishing one of her fantasy relationships was hers.

She sank deeper into the love seat, her legs crushed

against her, the heat from the pad easing the muscles in her back. The pain made the sting of the failed marriage deepen. It hadn't been that long before his affair started that they had tried for another child, somehow thinking it would draw them closer, but she had failed. The disappointment had actually pushed her further away from him and deeper into her writing.

She had left her children in the hands of her mother and their twice-a-week online therapist. She called every evening to say she loved and missed them and assured them all would be in order when they got back. In this way, she was left on her own with her bitterness and miserable thoughts. Her social media accounts had been smothered by pictures of her ex's wedding as all their combined friends shared pictures from the event. Melissa looked glamorous in her lace-and-satin wedding gown, her long, curled hair mingling delicately with her veil. Charles beamed at her, looking happier than he had in years. His scruffy beard was clean shaven, and his drooping, tired eyes were animated and alive. He was dashing in his tailored tux, proud as he leaned against a fancy limo, and exuberant at the reception, surrounded by all the things they hadn't been able to afford at their wedding.

Annie ran her hand through her dark pixie cut, which splintered out in spiky tufts, wondering if she should have grown it out like Charles had asked. But she felt good with a pixie cut. Even he had liked it—at first.

She gave her stomach a rub. Melissa was slender,

never having had kids of her own. Admittedly, Annie had dropped the baby weight in the past few years, probably because she ate like a bird since she was preoccupied with writing, and she had never been a big girl. Pudgy, maybe, and her stomach would never be like it was at nineteen, but she didn't think she was overall unattractive.

Her clothing style was made up of T-shirts and sweatpants, which her husband had once found cute, but he now preferred the put-together professional style Melissa wore, the one that looked like effort was involved.

Annie wasn't remarkably tall, not like long-legged Melissa, and her feet were embarrassingly small. Since she couldn't find shoes that fit, she often looked like a clown in oversized shoes. She could order the right size online, she supposed, but the effort it would take to send back things that didn't fit was too much of a deterrent.

Perhaps Annie should have tried harder to do anything except write. That was the only thing she could say was going well. That and raising her girls, but with so much of their time spent at school, it wasn't that hard to devote the few hours they were home in the evening to their care. No, her looks had nothing to do with his infidelity. It was the choice he'd made, and she had to live with it. She had been willing to admit her negligence and make it work. He still ran off. The blame was entirely his.

Tears welled in her eyes as she leaned into the cushions, imagining the couch as a friend letting her snuggle in for comfort, the way her husband had often done when they were first married.

It was too bad that night's dream hadn't been real. She sighed with longing. Sure, being in jail would have stunk, but then *he* came, and she could have stayed in jail forever with him. She felt a little guilty because it wasn't Charles, her ex-husband, she was dreaming about and longing for. It was Scott. It wasn't the first time she'd dreamed about him. And though it hurt, she hoped it wouldn't be the last.

Chapter 2

Scott stepped off the plane, sucking in a deep breath. The thick air of Norfolk, with its dense saltwater presence, was more than welcoming. He grinned. Though Ireland's air was also humid, it lacked the powerful heat the Virginia summer promised. The last two years had been a thrilling adventure. Better, anyway, than the eight years before, when he was married to the Marines. The Marines were a demanding lot—too demanding. The price he had paid was too high, though some of his comrades had paid higher.

He carried a single pack on his shoulder, and he was glad he was in civilian clothing. Too often in the past, well-meaning passengers would thank him for his service and pat him on the shoulder. He hadn't wanted the praise. He wasn't the one who deserved the glory. Instead of the slick Marine uniform he had used to please and impress his family, he now donned a worn-out pair of jeans and an untucked collared shirt with a T-shirt underneath.

Walking out of the airport felt a little surreal. It was

like coming home, except he was a different person. He wasn't Scott, the kid who had barely graduated, but Scott, the Marine, the world traveler, the experienced.

The air was heavy, the trees tall and lush, the sky—the little that could be seen—was cloudy, and the air smelled of the approaching storm. Rain and leaves twisted on the wind. He hoped it would be a Virginia thunderstorm—palpable, intense, and short, with a gleaming sun quickly following.

A familiar white car pulled in front of the building, and he chuckled to himself. Besides needing a wash, the car's paint was chipping off. The bumper was cracked in a few places, and one end was disconnected entirely. His mother honked the horn as she yelled a welcome out the window.

"There you are, Scott! Throw your stuff in the back and get in."

With a smile, he tossed his pack onto the back seat and sat next to his mother, sliding a few cigarette packages and fast-food wrappers aside.

"Hi, Mom. You know I can buy you a new car," he said as he felt a spring poke him from inside the seat cushion. "I have enough saved; it wouldn't be a big deal. It doesn't even need to be brand new—just nicer than this thing. I mean, I drove this around in high school."

"I don't want you spending your hard-earned money on me," she said as she lit a cigarette, tossing the lighter into the broken cup holder that balanced magically on the floor. The adjacent cup holder held her usual diet

Coke—she took a generous swig of it. "You earned it—you spend it. Besides, this car is still running fine."

Scott wasn't so confident as she shifted into gear and the car gave a resistant groan. "Are we going to make it home?"

"Shut your mouth!" she snapped, carefully guiding the car out of the airport parking lot and turning onto the main street. It was an hour and a half drive before they would reach Gloucester, a growing city, though still backwoods and spread out in the forests like an anthill, with only one way in and out. "I'll drop you off at your house so you can settle in, but you had better come over for dinner on Sunday or I'll tan your hide."

Scott snorted. He may have been on the leaner side compared to his buddies in his unit, but there was no way his skin-and-bones mother was going overpower his muscular body enough to tan his hide, though he wouldn't put it past her to try. He rolled down his window to allow the smoke from her cigarette to sail out into the stormy air. He had quit a while ago, but the swirling fumes tempted him to break his resolve of never picking up another one.

"You'll be at church, too," she ordered.

He almost asked which church, but stopped. It was too cutting. He knew she meant Catholic Mass at the church he had been raised in, but he had joined a different church shortly after high school. She conveniently forgot it every time he was in town, though he hadn't been back to his congregation in a long, long time. He had attended some Catholic Masses in Ireland, but it was more for the experience than it was for the soul-saving ordinances.

"I'll try," was his neutral offer.

"Hmm." She snorted. "How's it going with what's her name? Rachel?"

"Amanda," Scott replied. "We broke up."

"How long did she last? A month?"

"A week," he grumbled.

"There has been a Rachel, right? Scott, I don't mean to be *that* mom, but come on, son! You've done so many things to be proud of, but now it's time to settle down. How old are you? Thirty? It's really easy to get married nowadays. Of course, I'd like you to have a nice Catholic wedding, but we can do a quick something now and maybe make something bigger in a year. I'll need the time and all."

"Mom, I just got off the plane. I don't even have a girlfriend. Don't start planning anything."

She was silent for a moment. "Well, okay, but I'm not giving up on you. You deserve to be happy, and I know you've always wanted a family. What was it you used to say? You just wanted to get married to someone you kind of liked, work a job you hated, and have a couple of rug rats running around?"

"Almost. But I was being facetious, Mom. Pure sarcasm." It wasn't *all* sarcasm, but he couldn't say that to his mother. It might give her hope.

"All right."

The rest of the car ride was filled with his mother's

detailed explanation of what every member of the family and their shared acquaintances were doing. He zoned out, giving the occasional reply to encourage her to keep going. He stared out the window at the familiar sights of his old world. There were some changes here or there—new buildings for more shopping and the traffic was heavier, but the Coleman Bridge, Route 17, and the never-ending trees were the same, especially when his mother pulled off the main road and took the back streets, the hidden paths where all the people actually lived. He laid his head back on the headrest, wondering how the padding inside it could have moved to create an unbalanced lump on one side.

Turning into the driveway of his own house filled him with a little more emotion than he had anticipated. It was once his grandpa's house, willed to Scott before he passed. He had only stayed at the house a few times in the last couple of years, and it had been used more by his friends who needed a place to crash than by him. He had been too busy touring Europe and Japan. As his mother brought the car to a stop, he realized he would be alone, and he hadn't been alone in a safe, quiet place in a long, long time. His heart gave a lurch, and he shuddered as he shook it off, chasing out the demons that threatened to arise. He would not allow them in.

"Here we are," his mom announced after taking a last sip of her diet Coke. "Remember, Sunday dinner after Mass. When's your car getting here?"

"Joe's bringing it over later today," he said. "I'll be

at dinner."

He leaned over and gave his mom a quick peck on the cheek before getting out and grabbing his bag. He rummaged in his pocket for his keys, waving at his mom as she pulled out of the long driveway. He took a deep breath as he entered the house, pelted by the smell of aged dust and cigarettes.

It was just as he remembered it, with only a few signs that his friends had made themselves at home. There were some extra beer cans scattered around and cigarettes in the ashtrays, but it wasn't any worse than he might have left it. He dropped his bag and made his way to his bedroom. He had paid one of his buddies to put clean sheets on the bed before his arrival, and he was relieved to see a newly made, though sloppy, bed waiting for him. He never knew with his friends.

Scott threw himself on the bed, laying back on his pillow and swallowing the lump in his throat. He wasn't sure if he was glad to be home, but either way, here he was. He had spent two years wandering, traveling, having the best time of his life, but now he was home, unsure what to do with himself. The urge to go back out into the world was already twitching in his veins, but he had promised his mother he would stay put for a while, if only for six months.

Chapter 3

Annie couldn't stop thinking about her dream. She had tried reading, doodling, and watching some videos on her phone, but she couldn't shake the feelings the dream had given her. She sighed. It wasn't just the one dream. She had never told anyone, but she had dreamed of him throughout her marriage, though she had never harbored thoughts of cheating on Charles or seeking Scott out. He would just appear sometimes, often as a man in shining armor, whisking her away when things got rough. She had always assumed it to be symbolic, like a representation of unconditional love that she hadn't always felt from her husband—or anyone, honestly.

But this latest dream had been too much, as absurd as it was. It wasn't just about him, but about going home, getting back to what was familiar and safe, but also back to love. She knew Scott wasn't there anymore. He had joined the Marines and moved away, but she was still in love with the idea of him, who he had been when they were in high school.

She sat up, knocking over the empty carton of ice cream she had left on the floor, and wrapped her arms around herself. How she wanted to regain those feelings! She was used to writing romances, but all the characters were made up, psychological analyses of people and how they would react in strange situations. But she didn't want those. She wanted to be in high school–No! Not in high school, because that was an awful time in her life. She wanted to *feel* like she did in high school when she had spent time with him.

It was hard not to escape into her memories, to feel the unconditional love he seemed to offer her. She almost wanted to turn back time and run away with him instead, but knowing what she knew now, their marriage would have been a miserable one. If she could go back as the person she was now, she liked to imagine it would have worked out. Maybe if they magically crossed paths again, they would make it.

Annie flopped over the top of the couch, reaching over the foot of the bed, and dragged her laptop toward her before sliding back down, the warm heating pad keeping her spot toasty. She turned it on, entering her password with a flick and opening her word processor.

She was a swift writer. It was a skill she hadn't known she had until she started winning sprints at writing retreats—not by a few words, but by thousands of words. She graciously chose not to compete anymore so everyone had a chance to win a prize and stay motivated. She used her skill now, tapping out the beginning of the story she desperately wanted. It wasn't hard to recall the time they'd spent together and how she felt about the way he looked and smelled, though they had never really had a romance. It was the friendship and the promise of love that she wanted.

She would write about them, how they were. She would spend a little time reveling in the past since she was single, her ex was married, and her friend? Who knew where he was, but he was certainly not eating a pint of ice cream and writing stories about *her*. That she would put money on. So she began to type.

Though it was terribly cliché, Scott and Annie met at a high school Homecoming dance. It wasn't in a fabulous hotel or rented space, but in the much-too-small high school cafeteria. Annie, sixteen and far too insecure for her own good, had put in an immense amount of effort into looking nice, wearing a blue Oriental-style dress with slits up the sides and black leggings. The outfit had made her feel like Chun-Li when she looked in the mirror at home, but with no date and her confidence not even high enough to approach those she considered friends, she was certainly no Street Fighter. She stood by the side doors, glued to the wall, watching people pass, but mostly staring at the floor.

How she hadn't noticed him sidle up to her, she wasn't sure. Perhaps she had been too lost in her own forlorn thoughts to notice a stranger lean back against the wall next to her, folding his arms and peering down at her with quiet contemplation.

"You're Allen's sister," he finally said. This broke her reverie. She stared at him in surprise, then looked around to see if there was someone else he could have spoken to. Seeing they were alone, she managed a nod, if "nod" is what it could be called.

He continued, "Allen's a nice guy. He's in my biology class. He's kind of quiet, so I see the similarity. I'm Scott. Why aren't you talking to anyone?"

"I'm Annie. I don't have a date," she managed to squeak out.

He laughed. "You don't need a date to talk, Annie. You look nice and should be socializing. I'm sure some of your friends are here looking for you."

She nodded, pointing at some people she knew. "They're not looking for me. I doubt they notice my absence."

Scott turned so his side rested against the wall instead, the slight shift feeling a lot more intimate to the petite girl. "You should go talk with them. I have some people I need to find, but if I see you standing by yourself again, I'm going to have to ask you to dance."

Annie was sure he had meant it as a playful threat, as if dancing with a stranger was the worst thing ever, but her heart had started racing. A friend of her older brother's had talked to her, noticed her, the insignificant girl in the corner. The fringe of his clean-cut blond hair fell past his eyebrows, emphasizing eyes so clearly blue they pierced through her, persuading her that he could read her mind and know her secrets.

She wasn't sure whether to meet up with her friends or stay by herself, hoping to catch his eye and make him follow through with his threat. But the truth was, she didn't know how to dance, especially to rap music, and she was petrified that she would embarrass herself.

"Hey, Annie! What are you doing hiding over there?" Her friend Amber had left her group and made her way toward Annie with a grin. "Look at that dress! That is hard core."

Amber's dress was far cooler, Annie thought, with a spiked belt hanging over her hips and plaid skirt. "Did you just get here? We're hanging out over there. Come with me."

Annie obediently followed, standing in the circle and listening, rather than participating, to their conversations, her eyes wandering every few minutes in search of the boy who had spoken to her.

Though she looked around often, she didn't see him again.

Chapter 4

Scott scanned his dusty, cluttered house. Though it was late, he was too strung up to sleep yet. Doing a few things before bed would help him calm down, but he wasn't a great cleaner. He wasn't even a mediocre cleaner, but the thought had struck him that if he threw some things away, rearranged a few items, perhaps it would help him feel settled.

Though Scott's family had assisted in the clearing out of his grandpa's things, a lot of his grandpa remained. The majority of the furniture and dishes, the art on the walls, and even the towels were left by their previous owner. Scott wondered if making the house more his style would drive out some of the demons that hid in the corners and threatened to jump out. It wouldn't hurt to try.

He picked up his travel bag and lifted out his camera case, setting it on the kitchen table next to his laptop. He would update his travel blog later and post the last pictures he'd taken in Ireland. His photography had improved immensely during his travels, and he had taken to the idea of starting a photography business if he settled somewhere.

The rest of his bag contained his few clothes and some souvenirs that he could use as a starting point in making the house his own. He debated which room to work on first, feeling slightly swamped by the masses of clutter his grandpa had kept, even after they had cleared the house of so much stuff. He slung his bag over his shoulder and returned to his bedroom. That room wasn't overwhelming.

Scott took down the pictures his grandpa had hung by the window and tossed them on the bed. The lovely smoke stain left behind made it clear that a fresh coat of paint would be needed in the entire house, along with new carpets. He opened his bag and slid out the wooden Celtic cross he had purchased in Ireland. He hadn't bought it for religious reasons—more the thought that an Irish Catholic boy should buy a cross while in Ireland, even if he wasn't actively religious anymore.

The next items he pulled from the bag were a Hannya mask he had bought in Japan—he liked the idea of good luck in the form of a jealous female demon—and a small Eiffel Tower one of his dates in France had bought him. He placed the mask on the top nail already in the wall, making sure it was balanced enough that it wouldn't fall, before hanging the cross below it. Both were terribly crooked and not at all complemented by the smoky square outline surrounding them, but he could fix that later. He set the tower on the windowsill. There were a few more souvenirs at his mom's house that he would collect later, but for how, the room felt a little more like his.

He swung his closet door open. A couple of boxes rested on the floor, a solid layer of dust covering each. He grabbed the pictures off his bed and set them on the closet floor for now. He tapped his finger on the door, trying to remember what was in the boxes. They were his; his name was written clearly on the side in his own handwriting.

He knelt down and swiped his pocketknife across the tape of the closest box. He folded back the flaps and barked a laugh. On top was an illustration of him on a thick sheet of old art paper, his hand covering one eye in a ridiculously awkward pose his art teacher had picked from Annie's sketch book. Annie's hardly legible signature rested in the corner next to the teenage Scott, who sat at the imitation-wood table in the art room.

Picking up the old sketch, he couldn't help but smile. It brought back so many memories.

"I don't understand you at all, Scott," said Miss Andrews, the school's art teacher. She stared at him sternly from her desk since her leg was propped up, securely wrapped in a brace from a recent accident.

"It's an early class, and sometimes it's hard to get the

car started," he explained.

Her head rocked to the side as she tsked.

"Or maybe I sleep in," he admitted.

"That's probably more the truth," she said with a point of her finger. "Scott, you are a bright and charming young man with so much artistic potential. Why are you spending your time in corners smoking and skipping class? You already failed my class for lack of attendance last year. Do you want to do it again this year?"

He hung his head. "No."

"Good. Let's get you out of this school and on to better things. Right now, you have too many missing assignments to make it up in just the morning class. Do you have a free period during the afternoon drawing class to make up the work?"

He didn't, but his algebra teacher had already said that he didn't care if Scott showed up as long as he passed the tests. Algebra wasn't that hard. "Yes, I think I can."

"All right. Get caught up on the last three drawing assignments and then make sure you attend your class or I'll see you again next year."

With that threat looming over his head, Scott made the effort to attend the afternoon class, which, admittedly, was far easier to get to, so he really had no excuse. When he walked into the room, an odd thrill went through him as he spied the petrified wallflower from the Homecoming dance sitting with a couple of other students. There just so happened to be an open spot waiting for him right beside her. He invited himself to sit down, giving her a winning smile.

She stared at him in shock for a moment, unsure, it seemed, that *anyone* should be sitting there, let alone him, then said, "You're not in this class," as if to suggest he had lost his way and hadn't realized it.

"I am today." He took out his sketch pad, placing it on the table, then leaned his cheek in his hand as if waiting patiently for the teacher's instruction.

"You…" she mumbled, coughing to clear her throat. "I didn't see you at the dance again. Did you have a good time?"

No, he hadn't. He had become involved in an overdramatic teenage argument, and he had left early. "Yes, it was fine."

"You didn't keep your promise."

He glanced down at her, and she made eye contact with him. Was her smile a little coy?

"You said you would dance with me if I was alone," she reminded him.

He realized what she was saying. "I saw you again, but you were with your friends." He leaned a little closer to her. "But if you're upset about it, I'm sure we can make it up some other time."

"No, I was just joking," she said, turning to face the teacher, her hands sitting on her lap as she twisted her fingers together nervously.

Scott contemplated the girl. Had she been joking? Or had she really been hoping he would return to dance with her?

Annie's older brother was also dark-haired and quiet. Scott had managed a few small conversations with him over the years, so he knew a little about the family. Their parents were divorced, and the two kids spent most of their time alone, reading, studying, and walking in the woods. In the five minutes he had interacted with Annie at the dance, he had surmised two things—she was shy, and she was innocent, terribly innocent, more so than any of the people he considered friends who snuck in the alcohol and shared the cigarettes.

She peeked at him, probably feeling the weight of his stare. Her hazel eyes shone as she watched him, dark lashes framing the edges giving her a natural prettiness that was unaccented by any makeup. Her brown hair was tied at the nape of her neck in a long ponytail. Her shirt—which may have belonged to her brother, from the size of it—was covered by a black hooded sweater with holes that had worn into the sleeves. She had slipped her thumbs into those holes as if she was trying to hide every inch of her skin that she could. Perhaps she was insecure instead of shy.

"Today we're doing quick thumbnails," Ms. Andrews announced. "Jordan has volunteered to be a model. Now, this isn't the time for great details. This is meant to be a quick sketch to capture the overall image in a short amount of time. You will have ten minutes before he changes position. Then draw the next pose for another ten minutes. Did you hear me? Quick, overall shapes. Don't worry about the detail. Complete the entire person first!"

From the way she emphasized it, this had been a struggle for students in the past. In five minutes, Scott glanced at Annie's work and found her staring at the paper in frustration, her pencil sitting in the middle of the sketch as if abandoned mid-line. She had a complete sketch of the boy, with the start of details that she seemed to have remembered she wasn't supposed to do.

She caught his eye and gave a small shrug.

"If I'm not supposed to add details, I'm not sure what else I'm supposed to do with the rest of the time," she whispered. "Maybe I don't understand the assignment. Did I do it wrong?"

"It looks right to me. Do another sketch?" he suggested.

So she did. She had managed about three sketches in ten minutes before the timer went off and Jordan had to move to a new position, sitting in a chair, his legs spread wide with shorts too baggy. Scott glanced out the corner of his eye, relieved to see that from her angle, there was no risk of exposure of the boy's secrets, and she probably hadn't given it a thought.

This amusement proved too much for Scott, rising, folding his sketchbook, and leaning over the girl to whisper in her ear, "This angle is too close for comfort for me. One wrong move and it's all over. I have to leave that joy for you."

Her cheeks turned the most brilliant shade of red as she stared down at the table, the corner of her mouth curling in a tiny smile. Sneaking into her art class and seeing what surprises he could get out of her became his divine mission in that moment.

The next class created just such an opportunity. Ms. Andrews explained that her budding art masters would work up to oil painting, starting with thumbnails, then large preliminary sketches, before the final large painting. Each student had to provide ten thumbnails each for a landscape, still life, and portrait. He would have known the assignment if he had attended the morning class and might have had a plan prepared. Even so, he was clandestinely thrilled when Annie turned to him with a request.

"Can I draw your portrait?" she asked. "You're not supposed to be here anyway, and that leaves the other students free to do their work."

He wasn't sure if that was a logical argument or a dig at him, but he consented anyway.

Annie was swift as she worked, capturing him in ten quick poses. He never dreamed that the art teacher would choose the most awkward and uncomfortable one. Why he had even posed that way, he didn't know besides attempting to give the sketches variety. But he immediately regretted it as Ms. Andrews pointed to it and said, "I like that one because it's different."

There was a reason why people didn't use that pose and it was, therefore, "different."

"You'll be here next time, right?" Annie asked as the bell rang to announce the end of class. Though he had caught up on his assignments as quickly as possible so he could goof off as he pleased in this class, he had no desire to be a model in such a ridiculous and muscle-tiring pose, so he had strongly considered not coming.

Annie must have noticed his hesitation because her eyebrows knitted together, softening her face and giving her an edge of vulnerability. "Are you not able to? I wanted to do the preliminary sketch from life, but I understand if you can't."

"Yes, I'll be here," he blurted.

"Thank you, Scott!" She grabbed her things, hugging some books to her chest as she skipped out of the classroom.

He wasn't entirely sure how that happened. He wasn't accustomed to doing things he didn't like, but something about Annie's uncertainty and generous willingness not to hold him accountable as her model had affected him in a way that he couldn't explain.

Scott obediently stayed still during the next class, unable to watch the master artist work because of the angle of his face, but he still dared a peek every so often. A small crease appeared between Annie's eyebrows as she concentrated, making her look older than her round features usually did. She took on an air of confidence as she focused on her work, sat up slightly straighter, and when her gaze shifted back to him to reaffirm the details, he was struck by the mature, womanly face that stared at him. She apparently hadn't expected his wandering eyes and swiftly turned her face away, the woman retreating behind her pale blush. He found himself thoroughly amused by this discovery.

The following week, after their portrait sketches were done, the class was given permission to go outdoors without supervision to work on their landscapes with strict orders to return before the end of class, as Ms. Andrews's braced leg was sore and she couldn't manage the distance to chaperone them all.

Scott tried not to laugh as Annie dutifully gathered her supplies, which included a drawing board that was almost the same size as she was. She appeared so pathetically small as she clipped a few large sheets of paper on to the board, flung her messenger bag over her shoulder, and faced the door.

"I can carry that for you," he offered.

"No, thanks," she said, shoving the board under her arm. It was mere centimeters from the floor as she tiptoed to the exit in a lopsided attempt to get outside without dropping anything.

He was glad she couldn't see his look of amusement as he forcibly took the board from her arms. "Where are you heading?"

"Give it back. I can manage," she hissed, like she didn't want to attract anyone else's attention.

"And so can I. Besides, I need to do my sketch, and I would enjoy some company. Can we go together?" This wasn't at all true. He had, in fact, completed his sketches in the morning class and was putting off working on the oil painting until the teacher insisted, which might not even happen. Ms. Andrews had a tendency of avoiding enormous final projects with her students.

Annie looked like she was going to argue, her lips parting for the slightest moment, but then she gave a nod.

Scott knew the grounds far better than she did, for she had never needed to know where the choice smoking spots were away from cameras and teachers. He also learned, not surprisingly, that she wasn't inclined to sports, so he had the pleasure of introducing her to all the fields and outdoor areas from which they could pick their landscape sketches.

"Ms. Andrews seems to like things that are different," Annie said with a tilt of her head. "I wonder if anyone has ever painted a landscape while looking through a fence."

The two sat on the grass on the opposite side of the field where she drew the chain work of the metal baseball fence before filling in the gaps with the details of the field. When she finished, she merely turned where she sat a few times to get the rest of the thumbnails.

"Aren't you going to sketch?" she asked as he lay on his back in the field.

He dismissed it with a wave. "I'll get to it. What's your favorite book?"

"My favorite book?"

"Yes. I promised to keep you company, so I'm required to ask mundane questions. You carry books around. What's your favorite?"

She pondered a moment, looking up at the sky. "Have you ever read *Wuthering Heights*?"

"I can't say I have," he admitted.

"Well, that's my favorite book," she said.

"What's yours?"

"Hmm, I'm not sure. I've read a few I like. What's *Wuthering Heights* about?"

She was quiet a moment before she muttered, "A love triangle that goes wrong and turns into deadly revenge on the moors of England in the eighteen hundreds."

He gasped a laugh. "What?"

She flushed. "I shouldn't have said anything."

Scott pushed himself onto his elbows so he could look at her. "I have to say, I pictured you as more of a Jane Austen kind of girl, but okay."

She perked up. "Well, Jane Austen is wonderful, but there's something deliciously macabre about the story. I don't know. I like Emily Bronte better. Her sister Charlotte wrote *Jane Eyre*."

"Now there's a respectable book, if you favor the gothic style."

Annie's smile broadened. "*Jane Eyre* is excellent and most people prefer it, but I have to say my heart is with *Wuthering Heights*."

"Well, I'll think about what my favorite creepy romance book is and get back to you." He lay on his side, picking out a strand of grass and twisting it between his fingers.

She laughed. "First off, *Wuthering Heights* is not a romance. Second, you aren't required to like creepy books."

He cocked his head. "Do two characters end up together in the end?"

She hesitated, "Well, yes, but—"

"Then it's a romance. And I'm Catholic. I believe there's a bit of creepiness in my bloodline."

"Ah, from the Spanish Inquisition, perhaps?"

He huffed a laugh. "Touché."

The more he talked with her, the more he realized he liked the way she spoke. Her banter wasn't filled with malice or the delight of tearing another down, and he noticed himself adjusting to her style of speaking. She was unlike anyone else he had ever talked to.

Scott didn't realize it, but that was when he swiftly and unexpectedly fell in love with her.

Chapter 5

Annie stopped typing for a moment, stretching out her fingers and glimpsing back at the last section she had written. She was surprised at how easily she recalled Scott's visits to art class. He had always insisted that he needed to make up missed assignments, but now she suspected that he might, in fact, have been coming to the afternoon class to see her. She was so blind, and he was so reckless. He danced to his own drum in that school, wandering the halls as he pleased like a feral tomcat in the wild.

It was interesting. Annie remembered little about the teachers she'd had, her schedule, or the other students in her classes. Honestly, she could hardly remember what grade she had been in. She knew he was a senior, but what was she? A junior? The few memories she recollected from high school were mostly about him, and the reason she knew she hadn't been a senior was because he hadn't been there. He was the main protagonist in most of her high school stories. Even on usually uneventful holidays.

She typed again.

HE WILL NEVER KNOW

Valentine's Day was a particularly annoying day to Annie. The addition of the balloons and giant stuffed bears to the hallways as girls cuddled their boyfriends also caused them to stroll extra slowly and widely that day. Not that Annie wasn't a romantic—she had read *Pride and Prejudice* as often as the next nerdy girl had. It was the fact that she wasn't in a romance, or even close to one. Therefore, she had decided to take up a romance with learning, which all the new white, red, and pink traffic hindered.

That day she had PE, and she was convinced her teachers had taken great pride in embarrassing the awkward girl who couldn't recall the rules and didn't seem to understand how to use her feet and hands at the same time. After another failed session of whatever sport the teacher had tortured her with, she entered the locker room with the rest of the girls in her class, damp and defeated.

She thumped her head against her locker, wondering why PE was a required class and firmly deciding it was one of the few she would gladly vote to remove from school. She tugged her clothes out of the locker to change back into a normal human being, hiding the pale legs she had inherited from her father and the wide-hipped body she had inherited from her mother.

"Annie? Annie? Is there an Annie Johnson?" Her name echoed through the room. She looked up, met by faces that were saying her name and searching around, but not seeing her as if she was some invisible specter. She was the only Annie Johnson she knew, so she spoke up.

"Yes?"

"You're Annie?" a girl asked, stepping toward her.

"Yes."

"Someone's at the door for you." The girl pointed behind her. It wasn't the main door to the girls' locker room, but the locked-from-the-outside back door that led to the opposite side of the school for convenience.

Annie felt unnerved as everyone watched her walk from her locker to the door. It had to be her mom picking her up for a forgotten dentist appointment, or a teacher's reminder that she needed to attend the special choir practice. But why was everyone observing her with such intent interest?

A girl opened the door for her, much like the doors were grandly opened for a heroine in a fantasy movie, and Scott entered her line of sight, waiting, apparently, for her arrival, holding a single yellow rose.

She became acutely aware that she was still dressed in her gym uniform—black shorts and a red shirt, covered by her dependable hooded sweater with the holes in the sleeves. And she was terribly, embarrassingly sweaty, a combination of too much running and Virginia humidity. She wished beyond all wishes that she was wearing anything else. Scott was as handsome as ever, put together and accompanied by a light scent of cologne.

"This is for you," he said, holding out the rose like he

was passing her a pencil she'd dropped. "I chose yellow because yellow is the color of friendship, so you know it's not meant romantically. But I wanted you to have something nice today."

"Awww!" resounded from the crack in the door as all the girls in the dressing room, most of whom she had never spoken a word to in her life, reacted simultaneously to Scott's brief speech. She glanced back and saw at least twelve eyes peering at them. The flushed heat she already felt from gym class was intensified as she reached a shaking hand out to take the rose.

"I figured you wouldn't get much on Valentine's Day," he added with a gentle smile.

"You guessed right," she said, keeping her eyes firmly on the floor and hoping she didn't appear too drenched and disgusting.

"You look cute," he added. "I've never seen you in shorts."

Yes, she was ready to die now.

"Yeah, right." She pointed to the door. "I'd better change."

He nodded. "Yeah, see you later."

The door to the locker room, the supposedly locked locker room, magically opened again and she walked in, glancing back at Scott, who raised his hand in an absent wave before strolling along on his merry way.

Holding the rose in front of her, she timidly looked around at the girls watching her return. She accidentally made eye contact with a few, who winked and said silly things like "Get him, girl!" and she huffed a laugh. She couldn't "get" a guy who was bent on friendship. Even so, she was careful with the flower, setting it down safely while she changed and keeping it close as she went through her day.

Although the rebel in her heart refused to look on that flower romantically, the impractical part of her heart took that flower home and hung it up to dry. When it was a crisp version of its former self, she placed it in a vase and kept it in her room for a long, long time. It was from a friend, after all, so she could keep it whether or not she had a romance. And it survived a few failed romances.

She decided it wasn't fair that Scott could give her gifts. She wasn't a huge fan of presents. They impressed on her the responsibility to return the gesture, and if she knew anything about herself, it was that she was a terrible gift giver. Not just terrible, but shockingly and excruciatingly appalling. She thought she was a clever girl, but when it came to giving gifts, she over-thought it to where the item didn't even make sense anymore, and she had sworn to herself that she would never put herself in a situation to need to give a present again. But what Scott had done was so nice, she felt compelled by her sense of appreciation to give him something as well, even if she dreaded the idea.

One trip and many hours at the bookstore later, she had selected what she hoped would be a thoughtful gift. It was just a book, nothing grand, but she wrote a brief note in the front, signing it so he would remember who it was from, since she was sure there would come a time when he wouldn't remember her anymore.

She encouraged herself throughout the school day and stirred up her courage to give him the gift by reminding herself that it was the thought that counts, not the size or how sensible the item was, and any gift, barring something obviously foul and insulting, was generally received with gratitude. What was the worst he could do? She knew what—anything. Anything negative at all would crush her soul. But she tucked that truth aside and when they went outside for art class, she pulled the book from her bag and presented it as nonchalantly as he had the rose.

"Here, I got you a thing," she said, holding it out as they got to their usual spot and sat down, she on her knees, perhaps so she could make a quick getaway if needed.

"A thing?" he said with a chuckle as he took the book.

"It's nothing big. I just thought you would like to read it, since you're descended from creepy conquistadors or something and have creepiness in your blood, though I hope it's the right kind of creepiness."

"There's a right kind of creepiness?"

"Yes! Being interested in ghosts is quite different from wanting to create ghosts."

Scott nodded in silent agreement as he glanced at the book. "*Wuthering Heights*! Are you giving me homework?"

Her face flushed, and she wanted to crawl into a hole. Any hole she could find in this stupid field would do.

He noticed her face and laughed. "I'm sorry. It was just a joke. I'm really glad you got this for me. I was planning on getting a copy."

Annie nodded, not saying anything.

He flipped the pages before exclaiming, "And there's a handwritten note!"

"No!" she squeaked, sounding too much like the mouse she wanted to be right now, snug in its little hole in the damp soil. "Don't read it now."

"'Scott,'" he read aloud, "'In return for the rose, I offer you my favorite book with the humblest belief that you may find some delight in this macabre tale. Thank you for your friendship. Annie.'"

She crumpled to the ground, covering her face with her hands, forgetting she had positioned herself for a quick getaway.

"That's a sweet note, Annie. Why are you hiding your face?"

"I'm sorry if you don't like it," came the muffled reply. "I can get rid of it."

He tapped her on the back of the head with the book, and she immediately sat up.

"What was that for?" she asked, rubbing her head, though it hadn't hurt. She'd never had someone besides her brother do something so playful, and she wasn't sure how to react.

"Look, missy. If I didn't like it, I would tell you. Yes, I'm that mean. I love it, Annie. Thanks."

She nodded, hoping he didn't notice the tears she was

fighting back—tears of relief.

"So, I read that little book of yours," Scott told Annie at the next art class.

"How did you like it?" she asked.

"A lot, actually," he replied. "I liked the love triangle between Catherine, Heathcliff, and Edgar, though it's quite clear that she should have married Heathcliff and not Edgar."

"But I think Catherine was right about what she told Nelly. If she had married Heathcliff, they would have been poor and desolate. It was selfish to marry Edgar because he was rich. But Heathcliff and Catherine weren't ready to be together. I think they would have been miserable. Heathcliff wasn't successful yet, and it was her consideration of Edgar that made him change into something better. And what was she supposed to do when Heathcliff ran off? Besides, the ultimate point is that if they had forgiven each other instead of being selfish and bitter, none of the bad things they did to their families would have happened."

"I suppose," he said.

"Also, most people ignore the second act, and I think that's the most important part."

"With Catherine's daughter and Heathcliff's adopted son? I mean, that was a sweet ending, but everyone else was dead."

"It wasn't just a sweet ending. It was the redemption. Cathy and Hareton could have continued what Catherine and Heathcliff had started; they were also raised with abuse and neglect. But they chose to forgive each other. Because of that, the torments of the past ended, and Cathy and Hareton could live a happy life together."

"I like that. So, it's sort of a romance."

"It is *not*," she snapped.

"Perhaps not for Catherine and Heathcliff, though I love a lot of their lines." He pulled the book out of his bag, and she snorted a laugh as he opened it and she saw highlights and scribbles in the margins.

"What have you done to that book?" she asked.

"I like to make notes when I find things interesting. I've highlighted my favorite parts." He flipped to a page and read out loud to her, "From Heathcliff: 'Catherine Earnshaw, may you not rest as long as I am living. You said I killed you—haunt me then. The murdered do haunt their murderers. I believe—I know that ghosts have wandered the earth. Be with me always—take any form—drive me mad. Only do not leave me in this abyss, where I cannot find you! Oh, God! It is unutterable! I cannot live without my life! I cannot live without my soul!'"

Annie smiled timidly.

"What?" Scott asked as he noticed her expression.

"It's such a complex quote, isn't it?" she asked. "On the one hand, you want to admire the depth of his love, but on the other, you know that's not healthy!"

He nodded slowly, thoughtfully. "I hope to love so deeply that losing my lover would send me into madness. I would want her never to leave me, and if that meant a haunting, I think I'd be all right with it."

Annie went quiet for a moment, then replied, "I think I agree to an extent. I may want a true and deep love, but also a sane man. I hope that the man I love would not seek revenge in the way Heathcliff did if I refused him or died. I don't think a man willing to do that really loves. I think he just wants to own her, and it's not really love in that case."

"On that point, I agree," he said. "I much prefer Hareton to Heathcliff. Hareton loved Cathy in a healthy and just as endearing way."

Annie nodded.

"When I find someone, I will love them with my whole soul," Scott added.

Annie looked at Scott, surprised to find him watching her intently. Her cheeks suddenly felt hot as her heart beat painfully in her chest. As his blue eyes stared into hers, she found herself wishing that she was the one he was talking about. But she knew that would never happen.

"Me too," Annie managed to whisper as she broke her gaze, returning to her work, and fighting back tears that threatened to appear.

Chapter 6

Scott placed the sketch aside on the closet floor in his bedroom. It had made sense that he would keep it all these years, but he wondered if he should let it go now. This entire box was probably one he could throw out and not regret. Perhaps a bonfire? High school wasn't exactly his shining moment.

He looked in the box, and his eyes were immediately drawn to a small glass vial. He picked it up and sighed. What a silly thing to keep.

When Scott spotted the trinket in the gas station, he was struck with an idea. It was a tiny artificial rose suspended in a glass tube a little shorter than his finger. He smiled as he remembered getting her a yellow rose for Valentine's Day. Of course, he hadn't had the courage to get her a red one and proclaim his true feelings. She was a good girl, and he was not at all good. His past, short though it was at the time, was still too lengthy a list of foul deeds to recall. He was scolded regularly by his mother, priests, and teachers who had tried in vain to make him a better person. For him to court that young and innocent girl . . .

He huffed at the memory. Considering he was a bit of an old-fashioned romantic, he felt a wave of honor and self-sacrifice in leaving her be, probably from his Southern upbringing.

But he had wanted to pursue her, so he'd blurred the line in quite a clever way. Maybe too clever because it was clear from her reaction that she took it at face value—a yellow rose of friendship from her new art friend.

This rose in a bottle was the next step in his plan. Now that he had graduated and joined the Marines, he could make a move, a real move. He had cleaned up his act—quit smoking, quit drinking, and wasn't on the dating market. Now he didn't feel the guilt of corruption, and she knew about his past and didn't seem to mind it.

Beauty and the Beast was one of their favorite movies, so the rose encased in glass was perfect. It also had the advantage of being simple, with an undertone of romance. Friends give friends gifts when they visit each other. How was this any different? But his long-term plan of giving her a rose whenever he visited would become a visual of his feelings for her over time. When she was ready, she would see him for the chivalrous catch that he was.

As he drove to meet up with her, his thoughts wandered to why he hadn't made a move in high school. It was probably for the better, seeing as he hadn't lived his best life shortly after graduation, and he certainly hadn't kept in touch with Annie.

Growing up in poverty, surrounded by smokers and drug addicts, and raised by a single mother hadn't given him the best example of a good family life. His father had taken no interest in his upbringing, and he had no communication with him anymore. Though it wasn't great, this was the type of life he was content to have until he had met Annie. When he was with her, he saw something different. He didn't know how to have a proper, normal family, one that didn't do all the things that the Bible preached against. But she seemed to offer the promise of something better. She came from a broken home, but it had been a normal home for a while, and not one with any hint of smoke, beer, or violence. Her house had a feeling of sainthood.

When he pulled in front of her home, he took a deep breath. He had disappeared for a year after he graduated. Since his return, he had only seen her a few times, and this was his first proper move to winning her affection.

She smiled when she answered the door. "Hi, Scott!"

"Hey. Are you ready?"

"Almost. I'm just finishing up my piano practice. Would you like to listen?"

He looked awkwardly into the spotless house, unsure if he could really walk inside and not burst into flames, a sinner entering holy ground. "Yes. I'd love that."

"Come on," she said, taking his arm and guiding him down the hall and into the room that held a spinet piano.

She perched on the stool and placed her hands on the keys. With no book in front of her, she played a song that demanded her hands to dance across the keys with such speed, he wasn't sure how she didn't trip over her fingers as they flew.

When she finished that song, she turned to him. "I have one more to do. Is that okay?"

Yes! "Sure," he said casually.

Her hands returned to the keys and began playing a song in stark contrast to the last. It was slow and soulful, almost like a ballad, and Scott couldn't stop himself from reaching out and laying a hand on her shoulder. She jumped lightly, but didn't falter.

Suddenly, her brother Allen walked into the room, glancing around as if he was looking for something, and she sprang from the piano to greet him. "Allen, Scott came to see me, and he was letting me practice. I put dinner on the stove, and I'm going out. I'll be back soon."

"Okay," he said with a shrug.

Scott suspected she had moved so quickly because she was embarrassed her brother had seen them together. Did she think they were doing something wrong? Or had she disliked his touch so much that she wanted to run, but didn't want to hurt his feelings?

As they walked out to his car, he held out the rose vial. "I got this for you."

Her face lit up as he placed it in her hand. "Oh, Scott, it's lovely. What a sweet little rose. It looks like it's floating, doesn't it?"

"It's just a little something. I'm glad you like it."

"I love it! I'll be right back. I want to put it somewhere safe. Thank you!" She gave his hand a squeeze before running back inside.

That was the second time he had touched her that day, and he gave himself a mental high five. He was on his way.

Chapter 7

Annie sipped her hot chocolate as she scanned through the last section she had written, the light from the apartment window fading as the sun set. Those roses had been such a big clue of his feelings for her, but she hadn't noticed at all. Writing it down now made her realize how much of a young and naive girl she had been. Why hadn't he pursued her more openly? He was there, she was there, and knowing herself as she did, she would have fallen for anyone who paid her attention. With her own parents divorced and working too much to give her and her older brother much notice, she longed for affection. But he had never made an obvious move, thoroughly emphasizing their strong friendship, especially in high school, where they spent so much time together. Then he graduated and disappeared.

Annie's adult brain had to remind herself that things were better that way. After all, if Scott *had* made a move, she would never have married Charles—who encouraged her to be an author—and they would not have had Natalie and Rebecca. But her senior year had been a nightmare without Scott. It was hard enough to have parents who were neglectful and made Annie feel unloved and unworthy, but she made the mistake of dating the second boy who gave her any attention, seeing as the first, Scott, never asked to date her. Brent was short-lived, but he did enough damage to last a lifetime, and affected her idea of relationships for years.

"Gosh, Annie, don't take it so personally. They're just shoes. Don't be so sensitive," Brent said as he pulled her along the high school hallways.

"I did as you asked," she explained, fighting off tears. "I bought new shoes."

"But they're just as ugly."

She looked down at the brand-new sneakers she had bought after he demanded she throw out her last ones. They were more expensive than she would usually purchase, and she had needed to buy them in the kids' section because of her small foot size. Women's shoes bottomed out two sizes too soon.

"I thought they looked nice," she mumbled. "You said the other ones were old, and I thought that's why they were ugly."

"No, you're wearing boy shoes. It's stupid."

"But they almost fit, and they aren't covered in pink glitter."

"Pink glitter is better than those," he snapped.

She fell silent, allowing him to drag her along faster than she wanted to go. School was over, and everyone was making their way to the buses. Even though she could drive her own car, Brent insisted on picking her up, but that left her dependent on his timetable. Most days she didn't get home when she wanted, and he would fuss when she wanted to do an after-school activity, like trying out for the next play.

He stopped suddenly, shoving her into a dark corner of the hall. He leaned in to kiss her, and she turned her head away. "Please, not here. I don't like kissing in front of people."

"There's no one here," he said curtly. "And even if there were, they wouldn't see us."

"We can kiss when we get to your car." She tried to nudge him away playfully.

"I don't want to wait. I want to kiss you now." He leaned in again, and she allowed him a quick peck on the lips before pulling away.

"What kind of kiss is that?"

"I have to get home soon," she protested. "You know how my dad is."

"Give me a real kiss, like you mean it." This time he raised her chin up with his fist, holding her face in place. She squirmed uncomfortably.

"Brent, I really can't," she said, pushing his hand away. "My dad needs me home for a family thing, and I still have to stop by the theater. They're posting the cast for the play today, and I need to see if I made it."

He groaned angrily as he stepped back, grabbing her arm and dragging her roughly to the theater, where the paper she was expecting hung on the door. She ran her finger down the list and gave a cry of glee.

"I made it! And I got the part I wanted!"

She jumped up and down in her excitement, only to stop when she heard Brent say, "Dang it."

She turned to him. "What's wrong? I made the play. Aren't you proud of me?"

"Annie, you know I am, but I was hoping you wouldn't make it so we could spend more time together."

"We can still spend time together. It's only an hour rehearsal every day after school. There's plenty of time after that."

"Yeah, well, I'm going to get a job, so I won't be able to. That hour is the only time I'm going to have available, and you'll be spending it in there with those weird theater kids."

"They're not weird. And I'm a theater kid."

"No, you're my girlfriend, and girlfriends care more about their boyfriends than some school activity," Brent snapped before he stormed off, forgetting to give Annie a ride home like he'd promised. It wasn't a big deal, since she could walk, and she had lied about her father needing her. She had actually created a whole new father figure for herself—a father who paid attention to when she got home and grounded her if she was late. She had learned that Brent didn't like to hear no, and it was better to lie than to share her true feelings. She didn't enjoy kissing, especially in public. She didn't like being pulled around. But she did like it when he complimented her, which he did when she dressed a little differently than she was used to, and he spent time with her, even though he was busy. Very few people did, so he must care.

He had been extremely nice when they had first started dating, though that was becoming less and less frequent. She tried to excuse it as stress, with it being senior year and graduation was only a couple of weeks away. When he assured her it would get better because they could be together all the time, she gave him a fake smile while hiding her true feelings. She dreaded graduation for that very reason.

Annie stopped typing to wipe away her tears. It was easy now to see how toxic and abusive that relationship had been. It was by luck that right after graduation, Brent had gone to a training course in another state for the summer, and she had plucked up the courage to dump him. How she had found that courage, she didn't know. Desperation? Self-preservation? Researching how relationships are supposed to work and suspecting that maybe it was wrong? In any case, he had destroyed the self-esteem her parents had already left fragile, taken away any confidence that she was a desirable and worthy human being, and entirely crushed any ideation and desire she had held for a romantic relationship. She had seen her parents' marriage go down in flames, and after dating Brent, it was clear that she wasn't cut out for love.

She huffed a laugh. She recalled the out-of-the blue phone call that stirred hope.

"Hi. Is Annie there?"

"This is she," she replied.

"Annie Johnson?"

"Yes. Who is this?"

"It's Scott Candon. I went to high school with you," he said, as if she would ever forget.

"Yes, Scott! How are you?"

"How are you?" he asked nervously. "Is everything all right?"

Considering she had just dumped her boyfriend and was still spiraling, she was okay. Had he heard about that?

"Yes, I'm fine. Why do you ask?"

There was a slight pause. "I'm in town. Do you want to meet somewhere?"

She smiled as she felt a lurch in her heart. She knew he'd only ever wanted friendship, so she would never admit to him she'd had a crush on him ever since he had spoken to her at the Homecoming dance.

"Yes, I'd love to."

"Cool. I'll pick you up."

Though Annie was not one to get dressed up, she put on a nice pair of jeans with a T-shirt and her hoodie, the one with holes in it. She hadn't grown in years and it was still wearable and her favorite, despite Brent's attempts to throw it away.

When Scott picked her up, she was surprised that he wasn't driving his white car with the cracked bumper, but was driving a truck that glistened in the sunlight with all its headlights attached, unlike his old high school clunker. She was stunned by his appearance. His hair was no longer hanging over his eyes. It was short, but not quite shaved, which only made his eyes more visible and piercing than ever. He wore a T-shirt and jeans, but there was something startlingly different in his physique. He sat up straighter. His arms were no longer lanky, but toned, and he exuded confidence, much more than he had in high school. Back then, he was a slinking alley cat. Now he was a powerful Maine Coon.

"Hey," Scott said as she stepped into the car.

"Hi," Annie replied. "You look good."

"I was about to say the same thing about you. I recognize the sweater."

Though he smiled, she gave a self-conscious laugh. She probably didn't look that different from high school and she now wished she'd worn something other than her sweater, maybe something that would make her appear more mature and grown up, not an eternal youth.

The radio played quietly as they drove down the road.

"I was thinking of grabbing a burger. Would you like one?" Scott asked.

"Sure," she said. She sat back, feeling giddy. Though she knew Scott harbored no attraction for her, she couldn't help feeling the flutter of her heart. Something was different, and she couldn't quite place it. He seemed more mature and grounded, and it made her feel safe.

When they pulled into the fast-food drive-through, he ordered and picked up the food, then drove to a parking spot so they could eat.

She let him take a few bites before she began the inquisition.

"When you called, you sounded worried," she said.

"I did?"

"Yes, like you were concerned and checking on me."

He shrugged, taking another bite.

Seeing that he wasn't going to offer the story, she asked, "Why did you call me out of the blue?"

"Are you glad I did?"

She smiled. "Yes, but why? You must have had a reason."

He took a breath as he set his burger down and wiped his face with a napkin. "In truth, I called because I had a dream."

"A dream?"

"Yeah. That you died."

Chapter 8

Scott sat on his bed, staring at the box. All his energy for making the house his own was gone. He was feeling tired, probably from the unexpected number of memories and the emotions that came with them. Since that time, he had been all over the world, in the military and out. He was so far removed from his twenty-year-old self, it was almost like reviewing someone else's memories.

Annie. He had absolutely fallen for her, daydreamed about her and the life they could have. She had been the type who attended church every Sunday, and he had doubted she had ever kissed a boy. The only reason she had reentered his life after high school was his own foolish fault.

He had been out too late, drinking too hard, and his sleep was deep that night. His imagination had swirled between fantasy and reality, hardly knowing which was which. It wasn't until he was sitting with Annie, the girl he hadn't seen since he graduated a year ago, that he woke with a start. His dream had been scarily real. She sat right there, close enough for him to reach out and touch, her hazel eyes gazing up at him, and told him in great detail she had died and how it happened—a car accident just the day before. He had woken with a start, feeling sick and nervous.

Scott sat on it for a day, arguing with himself that it was just a dream—a silly dream—and it meant nothing at all. He wasn't a believer in premonitions; he put no stock in predictive visions. However, this dream had been so real, so incredibly unnerving, that he couldn't shake the fear that something was wrong in real life. And if it was wrong, he would want to know.

Making the phone call hadn't been too hard. She had the same house number she'd had in high school, and a quick search through a phone book—how old-fashioned—had given it to him. When making the call, however, his heart had been pounding more than it should have. What if it was true? What if it wasn't? How would he explain it to her? Would she be happy to hear from him?

The joviality in her voice, the happiness she seemed to have at hearing him on the other line, was intoxicating. How could she be so happy to hear from him? Didn't she remember how bad he was? And then he had the gall to ask her to meet him, and again, she seemed thrilled.

But when they sat in his car and she asked why he had called, how could he possibly answer? He supposed he could just tell the truth, in minor detail, and see what happened.

"So, you called because you thought I was dead?" she clarified.

"Yes."

"Well, I'm not, so that's good news, right?" she said.

She was clearly not dead. She was just as he remembered her. Was she some constant, impervious angel, some figment God sent to torture him for his misbehavior? Her long brown hair was pulled back into its usual ponytail at the nape, her bangs tucked behind her ears in a sloppy, though purposeful manner. Her clothes were thrown on, but fit well, and though she was small, she was by no means a child. And still a good girl—that much he could tell.

"You don't have to worry," she added. "I'm not mad at you."

"Why would you be mad at me?" he asked in surprise. He hadn't thought she had a reason to be angry.

"For not talking to me for a year and just disappearing. I'm glad you called."

Had she thought of him in the last year?

"I joined the Marines," he said. "I'm on leave."

"Oh," she replied. "That's good. My dad is military. I guess a lot of us around here are connected to the military with all the bases around. Where are you stationed?"

"South Carolina. It's not what I thought I'd do with my life, but it's not an awful choice."

"Not at all. I'm proud of you." Then she smiled, and

how grand a smile it was. He knew she didn't know him, the real him. She was still as naïve as ever, but he wanted her to think well of him. And he felt glad he had something good to report.

"What about you? Are you dating anyone?" Why, of all the questions he could have asked, did he ask that one?

She grew quiet, staring at the food on her lap. What had he said?

"I . . . dated a . . . not-great guy senior year," she said softly, ashamedly. "I'm only now realizing how bad he was. It's so stupid. He was so nice at first. I mean, really sweet. But over time, he made me feel awful about myself, as if I didn't already! Then he made me do things I really didn't want to do."

His eyebrows drew together in concern. "Like what?" He tried to keep the edge off his voice, but it was hard. He didn't want her to clam up.

"Like . . ." She looked outside the window, as if that would give her the words to explain. "He hated my clothing. He threw out my sneakers and made me get more girly shoes. He suggested I wear shorts instead of my 'ugly jeans.' He told me my arms were too fat, and I needed to work out more. Sometimes—this sounds stupid—but I felt like I had no control over my life. I wasn't good enough and I had nothing to offer. He said I was lucky to date him, and no one would ever want me."

"What?" That made no sense. "Why would he say that?"

"Because." She glanced down again. "I guess he didn't want me to leave him… I mean, he wanted to sleep with me, and I said absolutely not. He got really mad. I'm glad I didn't, but it's hard to think I'll never get my first kisses back. I cringe at the thought of someone touching me because of the way he treated me. I know it sounds dumb, but he knew how to tear me apart."

She went silent, her eyes looking anywhere except at him.

The anger Scott felt was overpowering. Though he thought he should say something, anything, to let her know she had done nothing wrong, he couldn't. He had the urge to break a neck, especially when he knew she had been kissed when she hadn't wanted to be. He wanted to comfort her, but didn't know how. He knew his silence must have made it worse, so he managed to get something out.

"Guys are jerks," he muttered. "Don't let them determine your worth. You've always been cool with me." Why *that* was the best he could come up with, he didn't know, but she still smiled. He couldn't help but feel a little guilt. Could he have stopped that idiot from being with her, had he been around? He couldn't hold on to what ifs. It was what it was, and all he could do was be there for her now.

Thirty-year-old Scott fell back on his bed. There were too many memories to recall. Why had he opened the box? It was like opening a chest of demons he hadn't even known he had. He had all but forgotten about her. She was a friend from the past, married with kids. He had stopped thinking about her the moment she said her "I do." He sighed. Maybe his mother was right. Maybe he had been running. In the eight years with the Marines, he had focused on work and getting through his deployments. The last two years he had used as a transition to cleanse himself of his time in the military. He had tried dating—a couple of girls in France, one in Germany, and even one in Japan, which was sort of fun with the language barrier. But nothing had stuck. None of them had the vision of the life he wanted. So, as his mother reminded him, he was still single and childless, two of the three things he had wanted all his life.

Chapter 9

Annie looked at the clock. It was five a.m. She had been up for twenty-four hours writing her story. She stretched, feeling the muscles in her back protest and the pop of her spine all the way down. Had she stopped for meals? Maybe one.

She had described the way they met, when he fell for her, some of the sweet things he had done, and how they had rekindled their friendship after a brief lapse. Now it was getting to the hard part.

She went to college.

For the first time in her life, she felt a bit of control. She had chosen the college, had a car that managed to run—though not over thirty on hills or in the mountains—and she was nowhere near the town where she had experienced so much abuse. She had a new roommate, Kristy, and they immediately hit it off. She was also seeing a counselor, which was helping her to see herself a little better. Scott was in the Marines and was assigned to a base in South Carolina, but it didn't feel far away at all. He had visited multiple times during his leave and called almost every day when he went back.

Of course, Kristy was intrigued by this mysterious caller Annie spent hours talking to at night. More than one time, Kristy had found Annie dozing with the phone next to her, like she had fallen asleep while talking.

"He's an old friend from high school," Annie explained.

"An old friend from high school? Like, your sweetheart."

"No," Annie said flatly, seeing as the only person she had dated in high school had been far from sweet. "He really is just a friend. He's made that very clear. But I enjoy talking to him."

"Hmm," Kristy replied, putting on a sly smile.

"Really! It's not like that!" Annie said with a laugh.

"Then why do you yell at the phone if he hasn't called?"

Annie's face flushed. "Because... the phone is stupid and not working right."

"Uh-huh . . ."

"It's true that . . . we appreciate each other's company, but I'm not ready. With what happened to me, I like the idea of meeting someone and falling in love. I like the idea of movie nights and long phone calls. I like the idea of presents on birthdays and dates in restaurants. But to trust someone with more than that again? To kiss? To marry?" She shuddered. "I don't know if I'll ever feel like a normal person again."

"I understand all that, and the counseling will help, but

he likes you," Kristy said. "Guys don't call girls they don't like."

"No," Annie argued. "We really are old friends. If he was interested, he would have made that move a long time ago. Like, years ago."

"I'm not so sure. Everyone is different. You have trauma—maybe he does too. But take it from me. No boy I have ever known has stayed up all night talking to a girl and not wanted to date her."

Annie shrugged her off. Kristy didn't know Scott the way she did. Kristy hadn't been there all the times he had insisted on just being a friend. And Annie didn't know what she would do if he wanted more.

Ironically, it was only a few days later that Scott made a move.

They talked that evening, like they always did. They told each other about their day and made a few jokes and laughs. When a lull took place in the conversation, Scott said, "I know I've told you this before, but I want to get married someday. I think it would be nice."

"Are you dating anyone? It sounds like you have someone in mind," Annie replied.

"I do," he admitted.

"Tell me about her."

"She's beautiful—"

"They always are," she teased.

"And talented. She's extremely smart and funny. I laugh with her all the time," he said. "I've hung out with her and I think we have something, but I don't think she's ready to hear that I like her."

"Scott, you're a great guy. I know you sometimes worry about your past, but that wouldn't stop any girl who really loved you. Why don't you ask her out?"

He was quiet for a moment. "Because it's you, and I don't think you're ready to hear it."

"What?" She almost dropped the phone. "What do you mean?"

"Annie, I know you feel broken, and I understand that. I'm willing to wait." He took a deep breath. "When you say you're ready, I'll marry you."

Annie's heart raced. He'd marry her? He'd take her away from everything? She wanted that. She wanted that so much, but something didn't feel right. As much as she wanted to scream "Yes," she didn't. Perhaps he was correct. She wasn't ready. But she wanted to be. Why couldn't she be?

"Thank you, Scott," was all she could say.

Twenty-nine-year-old Annie leaned against the couch cushion, trying to hold in her tears. She wanted to go back and tell herself to go for it, but even now she remembered how unprepared she was for that relationship. They weren't dating. They were in this weird limbo of no commitment. He was waiting for her to make a decision, and she couldn't even wrap her head around what he was promising and asking her.

She could see it from Scott's perspective. She hadn't said no. She hadn't said go away. If anything, she seemed to want to marry him. So he started making plans. He sketched out a ring he would get her, dolphins surrounding a diamond. He saved up time and money to go out and see her. He would romance her.

That was about the time she made her worst mistake, the thing she couldn't take back and that haunted her still. Scott came to visit her at college.

There was no talk of marriage. There was no pressure or expectations. He took her to dinner, where they reminisced, comparing times when they had goofed off in high school. Then they drove into the mountains to look over the valley and talk more. As the sun was setting, he took her home.

Scott had made no moves except to put his arm around her, which had been risky enough, and she had enjoyed the warmth. But it was she who raised her face for him to kiss.

Chapter 10

Scott hadn't thought about that night in a long time, but his mind wandered as he tried to sleep, clutching his blanket to him as he tossed and turned, trying to find a spot that wasn't hot or lumpy. Visiting Annie in college had been the biggest frustration of Scott's life for quite a few years after their parting, the unanswered question that repeated in his mind constantly. If she hadn't liked him, then why, why, *why* did she kiss him?

It wasn't just any kiss. It was a kiss that kept him up at night, longing for it. It was a kiss that was unlike any kiss he'd received before or since. He couldn't explain the appeal of it, the intoxication of it. Maybe it was just his feelings for her that made it so tantalizing. He had managed to get an arm around her, but it was she who looked at him with those big hazel inviting eyes, and she who had allowed him to lean down and kiss her. It was her hand against his cheek to draw him in, her lips that moved against his.

She pulled away, looking at him bashfully. Maybe he had misread it. Maybe he had made a mistake.

"Goodnight," he said warmly, trying to be casual, no pressure.

"Goodnight. Drive safe." She left the car, running to her apartment door and going inside with a wave.

He sat in his car for a few minutes, leaning his head against the headrest. He couldn't think straight, and he had to drive home.

Suddenly, Annie's apartment door reopened, and he watched her run out, rushing to his window and knocking on it. He rolled it down, wondering what he had forgotten or done wrong. But she said nothing. She only leaned over and planted another kiss on him, this one more passionate than the last. He wished the car door wasn't between them, but later thanked goodness that it was. He had the urge to run off with her then and there, to take her in his arms and never let her go, but she pulled away again, giving him a sheepish smile and a small "Bye."

The first kiss, he could have excused as a crazy-moment thing—maybe she felt pressured or was trying to please him. The first kiss, he could have dismissed. But it was the second kiss, the kiss that she didn't need to give him, the kiss that had made him lose his mind for a moment, and only a stupid seat belt and car door had stopped him from acting on it. That was the kiss that kept him up at night. That was the kiss that had convinced him her relationship with Charles was a flying fancy and he was the one she would choose. That was the kiss he couldn't understand. Why had she kissed him again? Why, if she had no feelings for him?

Scott scoffed. He only saw her once or twice after that, but there was no renewal of the affection she had shown that night. After that meeting, all she seemed to think about was Charles.

Charles was in the same English class as she was. He was premed and had to take the general education English class. They were thrown together for a group project and he came over to work on it. He was a good boy, like she was a good girl. He had no past and no clouds hanging over his shoulder. She felt no pressure from him and invited Charles to come watch a movie with her the next week.

Her introduction of Charles to Scott had started gradually. A brief mention of him during one of their phone calls, but that turned into a movie night. Then Charles stopped by every day. They went to a Halloween party as a goofy character of Annie's choosing, with other dates to follow—drives to the local smoothie joint, dancing at the school dance, and attending church together.

She would gush about how Charles was fun and smart, with no past to tell and nothing to hide. He was open and honest. Scott brushed this off, assuring himself that she hadn't meant it as a jab at him, but that Charles was boring. Then one day, she told Scott how Charles had confessed he was crazy about her. She realized he was everything she was looking for, and when she said her prayers at night, being with him felt right.

Making Scott understand that she had met someone else was harder than it should have been. At first, he didn't believe her. It was too fast, too soon. Then he humored her. He told her that when she had spent enough time with Charles, the flame would sizzle. But it didn't. What started out as flirtation grew into something more. They had become best friends, confidants, and she couldn't imagine her life without him.

Scott knew Charles had the advantage of location. Scott was too far to visit every day and worked a job that wouldn't allow frequent travel.

He tried to admit that she had attempted to let him down easy; he would acknowledge that much in her favor.

"I want to marry my best friend, the person I feel comfortable telling everything to and being accepted no matter what. I don't think we're that way," she said.

"I don't understand. We're as close to best friends as a man and woman can get. We talk all the time, and I haven't spoken this openly with anyone."

There was a brief silence before she continued, he could tell she was contemplating taking another approach at turning him down. "I don't think you really know me. I think you're in love with the idea of me, of who I was in high school. Sometimes you've said things that make me feel like you're talking about someone else."

"Such as?"

"That one time you described the ring you wanted to

get me," she said.

"The ring you didn't really have much to say about?" he asked.

"Yeah."

"What about it?"

She whispered, "I hate dolphins . . . and diamonds."

He scoffed, too upset to admit he was embarrassed that he hadn't known that. "It's just a ring. I can design something else. You tell me what you want, and I'll get it for you."

"That's not the point!" she snapped, which wasn't like her at all.

"Then what is?"

"The point is, Charles has asked me to marry him." She hesitated before adding, "And I said yes."

"Are you sure that's what you want?" he asked in disbelief. "Will he make you happy?"

She huffed a laugh. "No one can make me happy, but it feels right. It feels like the right decision."

He didn't know how to argue with that. "Well, if he makes you happy, then I'm happy for you," he said flatly.

"Are we still friends?"

"Of course. I talk to you because we're friends, not because I want us to be more."

She sighed in relief. "I'm so glad! I would hate to lose you."

But as time went on, Scott realized something. They couldn't stay friends after she got married. Maybe if he had been friends with Charles already. Maybe if he lived near them and found someone he could marry who wasn't Annie. Maybe if the universe wasn't set on torturing him. But he knew he wouldn't want his wife to be talking to another man, and he was sure that Charles would feel the same. She seemed naively oblivious to this fact, like Catherine in *Wuthering Heights*. She couldn't have both men. She couldn't have Heathcliff and Edgar too.

They continued to talk each night, Annie bombarding him with her wedding plans, school, and Charles. Though he tried not to, Scott was growing bitter. He tried to date someone on base to distract himself, with Annie's encouragement, but he soon broke it off. No one could hold a candle to Annie. Annie, who was making the biggest mistake of her life.

He tried to tell her so on one of the last occasions when he had visited her. He had picked the perfect road, nice and long, to drive on to convince her she was wrong. He had rehearsed what he would say and was sure it would work.

"Listen," he started, "marriage is just like driving down the road together. You can do it with anyone and still have a good time."

Annie scoffed. If she had learned anything about marriage from watching her parents, it was nothing like driving down a road together unless you counted car crashes as a normal part of it. It was work, and decisions, and fighting.

"Scott, I know what you're trying to do. I know you care about me, and I wish I could give you what you want, but I'm marrying Charles. I know it's right. I want great things for you, but I can't marry you. You must see that."

No, he didn't see that, but he didn't disclose it. "All I can say is, if you're going to marry that idiot, he'd better do his best to deserve you."

Scott was angry. He felt he had been robbed of something he had worked hard to earn. He had quit all the vices that any religion could say were bad. He had cleaned up his act, had a steady job, was clean cut, had joined a church, and the worst thing he could claim now was a propensity for swearing when he was furious, and damn it! If he couldn't have that, what could he have? Obviously not the girl of his dreams!

So he was not kind.

"Happy birthday, Annie," he said as he picked her up.

"Are you sure you want to take me? I told you it's unnecessary. I'm not offended if you don't."

"No, I promised."

"You promised before I got engaged. You really don't have to," she said nervously.

"I'm here and we're going," he said as nicely as he could.

He took her out to her favorite restaurant. She smiled at him, but looked tense, like she was waiting for him to snap.

"I'm working on a painting for Charles. What do you think?" she asked, showing him a picture on her phone.

He glanced at it, jealousy pulsing in his veins. "The

colors look funny. Are you sure you mixed them right? They look dirty and bland."

"Oh," she said, pulling the phone back quickly and checking the photo. "I suppose . . ."

"I just don't see what you see in him."

"I've already explained—"

"But he's so boring."

"Scott—"

"And he'll never care for you the way I do."

"Enough, Scott," she said, trying to stay calm. "I'm marrying Charles. Please don't make this harder."

"I just think it's too hasty."

Annie stood up, throwing her napkin to the table. "I'm done. Please take me home."

Scott knew Annie was angry, but he was seething. Why couldn't she see it? Why couldn't she wait a little longer? She had known Charles a few months. She had known Scott for years and still desired his company. What would she think of Charles in just one year, let alone a lifetime?

He parked in front of her house and she stepped out, storming into the house but waiting at the door for him to join her. Scott took a deep breath, taking out the book he had hidden in the glove compartment. He met her at the front door, stepping into the doorway and leaning his hand on the knob.

"I know we argued, but I appreciated dinner," she said, clearly trying to keep her voice calm. "It's a stressful time right now."

"Annie, I'm not trying to be cruel, but I need you to understand that I can't be there for you if you're with him. That's how it works. You have to know how much I love you. I can't stand by and watch you marry him. He would do the same if the situation was reversed."

"Scott!" she snapped. "I'm tired of saying this. I'm marrying Charles, and that is the end of it! He's my choice."

Scott nodded, letting out a remorseful sigh. "I hope you'll be happy, Mrs. Allred. Goodbye." His tone was as cold and harsh as he could make it as he shoved the book he was carrying into her arms and walked out, slamming the door behind him. Annie didn't come after him, begging him to stop, so he drove off without a backward glance.

She had tried reaching out a few times—texting, calling, emailing—but he never spoke to her again.

Scott got out of bed, picking up the box and taking it to the living room. He dumped it on the floor and started grabbing other items to put into the get-rid-of pile. There was a nice fire pit in his backyard. Whatever he couldn't donate, he could burn. He was sure no one would want that box except a small, regretful part of himself.

Chapter II

Annie cried. Oh, how she cried.

No, she still didn't regret her choice. Looking back, she would marry Charles all over again. But now, seeing the past written out on the screen before her, understanding better what she had done, she cried for Scott, for herself, and for poor Charles, who had been looking on at this baffling friendship and wondering why she talked with this guy, why she cried so hard when she lost his friendship, using the pages of a worn-out copy of *Wuthering Heights* to catch her tears. She had given up Scott for Charles. And now she had lost both.

Suddenly, she realized her life had played out like *Wuthering Heights*. It was not a romance, but a horribly, deliciously twisted tale of revenge. Annie had never sympathized with selfish Catherine or vengeful Heathcliff before, though she saw more of Catherine in herself than she would like to admit. She recalled a line from Catherine about Heathcliff that suddenly resonated with her and her feelings toward Scott.

> He shall never know I love him: and that, not because he's handsome, but because he's more myself than I am. Whatever our souls are made out of, his and mine are the same.

She read through her book in tears, seeing how clearly he had viewed himself, why he might not have made a move in high school and how hard he had worked to clean himself up, surprisingly like Heathcliff did for Catherine. But she wasn't ready for him. She wasn't ready for the worldly Scott who carried around his own scars. She wasn't unbroken yet. Scott didn't know that. Charles was her Edgar Linton. Charles was what she needed at the time. And Charles, in his own way, had deserved her. It was Charles who had made her go to counseling to heal. It was Charles, as inexperienced in the world as she was, who had allowed her the space to grow and had grown with her, and it was Charles who had encouraged her to follow her dreams and become an author. But now Charles was gone. They had let their ten-year marriage die. The vehicle from that easy car ride Scott had described had broken down on the side of the road, and though she had been willing to fix it, Charles was not.

He had been there for her, but she hadn't been there for him. She had truly been a Catherine to her Edgar, selfish and unfeeling in the end, only worried about her needs and the world she wanted. Charles was wrong and shouldn't have strayed, but she hadn't appreciated him while he was there. She had needed another lesson—

never take another person for granted. She had written her books, built up her career, and lost her husband. Now she needed to pick herself up. She had to move on from Charles. Unfortunately, her Heathcliff was also gone.

It was strange that she had dreamed of Scott. She had not seen or spoken to him since her marriage, and yet she felt as close to him now as she did then. But that was ridiculous. He probably hadn't given her a second thought after he had said goodbye. She knew he had dated a couple of people during her engagement—perhaps he had married one. What was it he said to her once? "I'm a simple guy with simple wants. I just want to marry a girl I barely like, work a crappy job, and have a couple of rug rats running around. Is that so much to ask?"

It was a joke he'd made in observation of what he had been raised with, but it was the core of what he had really wanted—a family, different from the one he had been given. The one with a father and mother, kids, a steady job, and a home.

Annie sighed. But what if Scott hadn't gotten married? What if he was secretly waiting for her? What if they met again, and he married her now, when she was ready? Was Heathcliff out there, wishing his selfish Catherine would come back and haunt him?

Annie had written their past romance and gotten it out of her system, but what if there was another ending she could write for them? She could indulge her feelings and her imagination. He would never be the wiser, Scott with his seven kids, super-hot wife, and enjoying the knowledge that she had been dumped by Charles like she had dumped him. Well, he probably didn't know about Charles, but still.

She stretched, took more ibuprofen, did some jumping jacks, then sat back down, moving the heating pad to her stomach and enjoying the warmth on both sides of her body.

Then she wrote, and wrote, and wrote deep into the morning. She knew she would have to sleep at some point and was glad the children were with her mother so she didn't need to stop. She immersed herself, wholly and happily, into the fairytale romance of herself and Scott. It had been a different romance than the one she'd had with Charles. It was deeper, more passionate, and made her, for that morning and afternoon, feel more whole than she had in a long time.

Annie got to say all the things she had never said out loud, explained all the mistakes she made, all the reasons why it was better this way. They were mature now, able to see each other as they were. They were ready for this second, more complex romance, and they didn't regret the past. They rejoiced in it because it brought them together at the right time. And that was how she ended her romance novel. Catherine and Heathcliff were reunited at last.

She slept deeply for the next twelve-ish hours. And she dreamed of Scott again. Only she wasn't in a jail—she was sitting in his car, snuggled against him in front of her apartment and turning her face up to give him a kiss. And when she returned for the second kiss, he got out of the car, lifted her in his arms, and never let her go.

"Aaliyah, I have a new manuscript for you," Annie reluctantly said to her editor only a day later.

Aaliyah's red lips filled the screen of Annie's phone with an ecstatic smile. She clapped in delight, her computer screen shaking, causing her abundance of obsidian curls to blur into one dark mass.

"Oh, that's wonderful news, Annie!" Aaliyah exclaimed, her Southern accent more obvious than Annie's, having come from Louisiana rather than Virginia. "You know, I've been so worried about you with Charles remarrying and everything, but I'm glad to hear you've been working! I can get that baby back to you in three weeks and then we can plan for a launch in another month if you have a cover ready. What's the setting? France? New York? A romance again? Those are my favorite."

"Uh, no, I'm not going to publish this one," Annie said. "It's a dumb writing exercise, and you'll see why when you read it. I want to make it nice for myself—a guilty pleasure, if you will. I let out a lot of emotions, you know, and just want it looked over."

There was a moment of silence. "I'm getting paid, right?"

Annie laughed. "Yes, of course."

"Okay, so why aren't you publishing it? I'm confused."

Annie sighed. She couldn't go into it with Aaliyah, though she was probably the person who would understand best, and the only reason she trusted her to see it. "Just read it, edit it, and you'll see why."

Aaliyah grunted a laugh. "All right. I get it. I'll still need three weeks to get it done, though, Sugar. You know I don't halve anything."

"I know. I don't want halves. I want your best work, but it's just for me this time."

"You got it. Send it over."

Chapter 12

Scott was satisfied as he sat on his new couch. It had taken all week, a couple of bonfires, and four trips to the thrift store in his pickup, but he had cleared out most of the stuff he didn't want and replaced it with a few choice items of his own. The couch was his. His new couch. A couch a man could be proud of. It had a drink holder on one side and a slot for a remote on the other. He had thrown out the beer cans and ashtrays, though the walls were stained with smoke that was very apparent when he had taken down the neon beer sign and a few bikini models his friends must have put up after he was gone. The walls were getting cleaned up, and with a few coats of paint, they would be as good as new.

His bedroom was clean, and the bed was made. His shirts were hung up, and there was only one box hidden in the back of the closet—a box he didn't think about, but would burn when he got the chance. The other bonfires hadn't been a convenient time. They had too much in them already. He had been sure the fire department would show up at any minute, with how big they were.

Yes, he would burn it . . . later.

He checked his phone. Sunday dinner was in an hour. Reluctantly, he rose from the couch and entered the bathroom. Despite his mother's opinion, the scruff looked good on him. Or at least, that's what he told himself so he wouldn't have to shave. He brushed his teeth, then stepped into the bedroom.

He pulled out a clean collared shirt, ignoring the box that peeked out from the closet, and made his way to the car. It wasn't long before he was out of his driveway and in his mother's, his music blaring so loud, he couldn't think. He liked it that way.

The trailer his mother owned was in the same condition it had been in when he had last seen it. He had offered to buy her a new house as well—even presented her the one his grandpa had left him—but she had refused. She liked what she had and where it was located, and that was that.

Scott entered without knocking, calling for his mother as a way of announcing himself. The mouthwatering scent of sausage and roux filled the house. His mother had prepared breakfast for dinner.

"Hey, Scott, biscuits and gravy are ready," she said, setting the bowl of biscuits on the table with a couple of plates and forks. He gladly sat at her dinner table, helping himself without another word. "Ah!" she snapped, slapping his hand. "Grace first."

He tried not to grumble as he allowed his mother to say a quick prayer before they ate.

"When are you going to shave that beard of yours?" she started as he took his first bite. "I'm not saying it looks bad. I just think you look nicer with a cleaner shave."

Stroking his beard, he replied. "I think it makes me look distinguished. It's all the rage in Ireland."

"It's all the rage here too, but that doesn't mean you need to have it. How will a nice girl fall for you if she can't see your face?"

He grunted a laugh. "Men with beards get married all the time. It's not that strange."

She shrugged in defeat. "Tell me about your latest trip. How was Ireland?"

He realized he'd left his camera at home, so he couldn't show her the pictures. "It was beautiful. Later I'll send you some shots I took. I was almost tempted to stay for the long term."

She choked on her food. "Long term? You'd just abandon your mother like that?"

"I came back, didn't I?" he said, spreading out his arms. "I stayed with some cousins for a little while, and by the end, it wasn't too hard to understand each other. I was thinking that with some practice, I could sound like a native when I go back."

"Go back? You're not traveling again, are you?" Her voice was tense. She was trying to be lighthearted, but she was really getting angry.

"I'm thinking about it," he answered defensively.

"Scott." She laid a hand on his knee, her tone taking on the serious mother edge that meant he was about to get a heaping of reality and he wasn't sure he wanted to hear it. "You were in the Marines, and you've been traveling all over the place for ten years. That's all fine and dandy. I'm glad you've had a good time and I hope you found yourself, but it's time to stay in one spot for a little while. Take a breath, work a normal job, meet people—"

"Settle down, get married, give you grandkids. Is that where this is going?" he said with a rueful smile.

"No. Yes, I want that, but as much as I'm proud of you and have seen you grow into a fine young man, I sometimes wonder if you've been running from life rather than living it."

Scott scoffed, frustrated to hear all this again. He put on his bravest face. "Mom, I'm fine. You're right. I'll stay put for a little while. This week I unloaded the house of Grandpa's things. I'll spend the next month fixing it up."

"Good. I don't mean to harp on this, but I do want to hear you're getting out and meeting people. Don't coop yourself up out there. I want you to date and get comfortable, find someone nice who brings out your best, but I want you to feel settled more than anything. I want you to be home and happy."

"All right, Mom," he said, gathering a forkful of biscuits smothered in gravy. "I'll get settled in."

Scott stared at the app he'd downloaded. There were a million of them, it seemed, all for meeting your soul mate. He could click, swipe, thumbs-up, wiggle, and who knew what else to meet someone who did the same back. He typed in some information for a profile, jotting a few dreary words about himself. *Marine vet. Never married. Intelligent. Woman must like dogs and travel.* That fit for now.

He lay on his bed, swiping pictures of different girls. Some were okay-looking—some profiles were hardly decipherable. He wasn't that old, but some of these girls looked like babies. In the end, there were only two that he marked as interested, and only one who responded.

Elizabeth.

Chapter 13

A lot can be accomplished in three weeks. After sending her book to her editor, Annie Allred, formerly Johnson, was feeling strangely well. She no longer felt the need to cry and cuddle her pillow at night. She made her bed when she woke up. She had breakfast every morning, lunch and a snack, and took herself out to dinner in the evening. She outlined a couple of new books, found a nice-looking house to rent with two bedrooms, plenty of room for their books, and a spacious backyard. She even purchased a few pieces of furniture. As it was, she hadn't needed the studio apartment for the entire three weeks while she was waiting for the manuscript, and was singing to herself as she hung her daughters' wall decorations up in their room when her phone rang. She managed to answer it and put it on speaker without dropping the nail and hammer.

"Hello?"

"Hello, Mama!" Aaliyah's voice echoed through the room. "How's it going?"

"Really well," she said. "I moved into our new rental,

HE WILL NEVER KNOW

and I'm decorating like a happy housewife. Well, house . . . divorcee?"

"Ha! That's right—own your status. You sound great."

"I feel great. So, what's up?"

"Enough with the small talk, right? So, here's the deal. We're publishing this, babe."

Annie was glad the phone was on speaker because she definitely would have dropped it. She dropped her hammer instead, picking up the phone and taking it off speaker. This was a wander-around-the-house type of phone call.

"What? No, I said we *weren't* publishing it."

"I know that's what you said, but it's what's happening. The world needs this story. I was up crying and laughing way into the night. My husband hit me with his pillow so many times, I had to confiscate it *and* his phone. Who does he think he is, telling me I can't read, but he can watch his football all night? Telling me I'm too loud . . . Anyway, I couldn't put it down. We must publish it! This is the best thing you've ever written."

"You don't understand. This is a true story with a fairytale ending about an old friend from high school. I can't publish it. I don't think that's legal."

"Sugar, it's a romance. No thirty-odd male is going to be reading it."

"But my friends might read it and realize it's about him. I mean, I didn't even change the names. I should look into it."

"That's fine," Aaliyah said nonchalantly. "Look, I

thought you might be this way, so I already looked up the laws. You have nothing in there that's illegal."

"Really?" Annie asked. "Because some things are really specific. Couldn't I be sued?"

Aaliyah waved it off. "No, you're good. Keep the first names the same. I love them, and you can't sue over that. Change the last names—they only appear like twice. To make you feel more comfortable, I think we could publish it under a pen name."

Annie ran her hand through her hair, ruffling it like agitated chicken feathers "A pen name? I wouldn't have any publicity."

"That's the beauty of it. We make you a debut author promoted by a fellow author who loved her book—AKA you, so you don't lose your platform—and even joke that she stole your name. It's fantastic!"

"You're my editor, not my publicist." Annie laughed.

"You're lucky I don't charge for my ideas. Listen, I have a passion for this project, and I want to be with you every step of the way. We're getting this out there, and you are going big."

Annie tapped her nails against the door frame as she thought about it. A pen name would be an excellent cover, and authors supported each other all the time, and having someone encourage and push her through the process was something she missed now that Charles had left.

"I don't know . . ." What were the chances that Scott would read the book? Aaliyah was right. Not only was he who-knows-where, but he certainly wasn't in the middle of Arizona checking out new release contemporary romances about second chances. He wasn't even on her social media pages, not that she had checked or anything . . .

"Come on, do it! Be bold! You're an author, and you killed this. With a swift edit, we can get it out. I know you have your usual cover artist, but I have another gal in mind who could create the perfect cover at a reasonable cost. I'll email her portfolio link so you can check her out."

"I mean, if you're that passionate about it . . ." Annie mumbled.

"Oh, I insist. I've already emailed you the notes. A few minor tweaks, a closer look at his character development, but overall, I'm in love."

Annie couldn't believe what she was hearing. Aaliyah was not one to mince words. If she thought it needed to be published, then she supposed published it would have to be. Honestly, who was it going to hurt? It would be just another cheesy romance novel like all the ones she had written before. Only she would know the truth, and that kind of made her giggle.

Chapter 14

Scott sat at the table of the restaurant Elizabeth had chosen. Williamsburg was the perfect place for a first meeting. A great backdrop—not too crowded this time of year, but still public. The aged buildings were scenic, and the flowers filled the air with a refreshing scent. He didn't need to feel nervous about meeting a complete stranger, one he had mild hopes would be the girl of his dreams so he would marry, have kids, and his mother would stop whining at him all the time. No pressure.

He looked at his phone, swiping through texts from his buddies who were looking for a place to crash during Thanksgiving. Perhaps he would let them stay at his place while he went out of town for a week. He could charge them like a real Airbnb rather than letting them drip beer on his carpets with no consequences. He'd have to ban indoor smoking. That was fresh paint, and he was having the carpets replaced soon. His house would smell like his cologne and not an ashtray.

"Scott?"

He glanced up and immediately recognized Elizabeth from her photos. She wore form-fitting jeans and an oversized shirt that hung off one shoulder in a flirtatious manner. Thank goodness he hadn't been catfished.

"Elizabeth?" He stood, sticking out his hand for a firm handshake. He realized that might be too formal. This wasn't a job interview. Would a hug have been more appropriate?

She laughed as they fumbled for a weak handshake instead.

"Sorry," he said, indicating for her to take a seat. "It's been a while since I've done this."

"I understand," she said. "I rarely go on to these dating apps, but I was free for the weekend and thought, why not?"

"Exactly."

"So, you're a travel photographer?" she asked, sweeping her gently wavy hair over her shoulder and leaning on her hand. She had perfectly selected makeup to accentuate her face—a light smoky look, not too heavy like some of the raccoon ladies he had seen, but blended seamlessly. Her eyes were a deep brown that seemed to glow.

"Not exactly. I was a Marine for eight years, and when I got out, I took up photography, traveled around, and started a silly travel blog."

"I know. I checked it out."

"You did?" he asked.

"Oh, yeah. It was super easy to find. You have quite

a talent. I feel like some of your pictures should be in *National Geographic*."

He shook his head, holding up his hands so she wouldn't get the wrong idea. "Not quite, but I appreciate the compliment. So, you know all about me now."

She laughed, throwing back her head, then tapping him lightly on the arm. "I'm sure there's more to you than that!"

"That sums me up. What about you?"

"Right now I'm studying for my master's in anthropology at William and Mary."

"Oh, wow. Well, I'll see my way to my car," he said as he rose.

She placed a hand on his shoulder and pulled him down with a giggle. "You're not intimidated by smart women, are you?"

"No, I just don't have anything interesting to say. I'm sure you've heard all the jokes and cheesy pickup lines. I'm afraid I haven't prepared myself for this."

"Well, if I think you have potential, you can study up for our next date. I can't imagine there are too many pickup lines for an anthropologist."

"We men are pretty savvy. We can make a pickup line out of anything. I'll impress you next time. What do you want to do with your degree?"

"I want to spend some time in Egypt contributing to the excavations there. I've always been fascinated by Egyptian history. After that, I'm not sure. I figured I would go from there."

Scott nodded appreciatively. "So, you're interested in old, stale corpses? That would be why you swiped on my photo."

"No!" she said, smiling. "Actually, it was your profile description. 'Marine vet. Never married. Intelligent. Woman must like dogs and travel.' Concise, no nonsense. I liked it. Much better than 'one-night stand' or 'I'll rock your world, baby.'"

"Well, at least I don't come off as creepy."

"It's surprisingly hard for a man not to do on dating apps nowadays."

He sat back and sighed. "I haven't gone to Egypt yet. Europe and Japan were my hits."

"That's still very impressive. I appreciate a well-traveled individual. I feel like most people don't get out of their bubbles enough."

"That is true," he agreed.

"I'll be done with my masters in December, and I'm working on my papers to join an excavation. My professor is sponsoring one with her colleagues at Oxford, and she said she wants me on her team. It's really exciting."

They were interrupted by their server, and they stopped talking to order.

Scott glanced at Elizabeth while she perused the menu. This restaurant was a frequent haunt of his, and he already knew what he wanted to eat, so he took the opportunity to admire the young woman. She wasn't that much younger than him, but she was vibrant and full of life. He had never considered traveling to Egypt, and she intrigued him. She wasn't the typical girl he was used to dating. Elizabeth was refreshing, like a tall glass of hope.

Chapter 15

"What do you girls think?" Annie asked.

"It's awesome!" the girls cried as they bounced around their room.

"All our stuff is here," Rebecca said, stroking everything she recognized as hers. "I thought it was all lost in the divorce."

"Oh, no, honey," Annie replied, getting down on her knee to be on eye level with her seven-year-old. "The only thing that was sold was the house. All your things are still yours."

Rebecca nodded, then jumped onto the bunk bed she would share with her sister.

Natalie sat quietly on the chair at the desk, looking around as if contemplating every detail of the room. It wasn't her old room, the room she had grown up in and hadn't needed to share, but Annie hoped her too-mature nine-year-old would see past that. She wanted them to heal.

"Girls," she said, sitting on the bottom bunk and waving her arms for them to join her. When they sat, she took a deep breath. "I know things have been hard for you. Your dad and I decided not to be married anymore, but that had nothing to do with you."

"Yeah, that's what Miss Sandra said. We get it," Natalie said.

"Your counselor? Do you like her?"

They both nodded.

"She told us that our parents love us very much and we can still be a happy family, just a bigger one," Rebecca chimed in.

Annie smiled eagerly, sliding off the bed and kneeling in front of them so she could see their faces. "Yes! That's right. I know you two like Melissa."

Natalie shook her head. "We don't, Mom. I promise."

"Oh, honey." Annie placed a hand on her daughter's cheek. "You don't have to lie to me. Melissa is very nice, and I like her. I want to welcome her to our family."

"You do?" Natalie asked.

"Yes. Sometimes things happen that we don't expect, but we can choose how we react to it. Daddy, who we all love—"

"Do you love Daddy?" Rebecca asked.

Annie knew she had to tread carefully. "I love Daddy in a new way. He's like my best friend, and he has given me a new person to be friends with. It's not what I wanted, but I can choose to be happy or I can choose to be sad. You girls don't need to choose between me and Melissa or me and Daddy. We can all love each other and be a big, happy family."

Tears welled up in Natalie's eyes, and Rebecca, seeing her sister in tears, followed suit, throwing her arms around Natalie. Annie wrapped her arms around both of them, taking deep breaths of her own.

"I have some news," Annie continued, talking into Natalie's hair. "School starts in a week, and Daddy has asked if you would like to spend some time with him and Melissa."

"I don't want to leave you alone some more," Rebecca said, pulling away and wiping her cheeks, which somehow created a streak. Annie laughed and rubbed it away with her sleeve.

"You girls will be with me all school year. And I'm not alone. I have your love, and knowing you're spending time with your daddy and getting his love makes me so happy." The girls crushed her in another hug. "And I have a new book out."

"Hurray!" the girls said in unison.

"Would you like to see it?"

"Yes!"

Annie had always made a point to involve the girls in her writing adventures. They couldn't read the romance books until they were older, but she had written a few children's stories just for them, and they had caught the writing fever. Now they wrote their own books and shared them with her as well. It was their thing.

She led them to the living room, pulled her book off the shelf, and handed it to them.

"Oh, the cover is so pretty," Natalie said as she stroked

it. "But your name isn't Catherine A. Linton."

"Yes, it's a pen name. It means I'm pretending to be a different person. It's a different book than I usually write, so I felt this was best for it."

"Oh," Natalie said.

"My pen name would be Pirate Octopus," Rebecca announced.

"I like it," Annie said. "So, while you two are with your father and getting to know your new stepmother, I'll be doing a book signing in Phoenix."

"I want to come," Rebecca cried, beating Natalie to it, who nodded in agreement.

"No, it would be so boring for you, and you need this time with your dad. But I'll tell you all about it, and if he says you've been good, I might bring you back a book or two."

"Oh . . .okay," Rebecca said.

Annie could tell Natalie was already choosing the books she wanted in her head.

"The campaign went really well, Aaliyah."

"Don't I know it!" she cried, her screen going crazy as it moved around while she spoke over video phone.

"I assume your enthusiasm isn't just about sales. What's going on?" Annie asked. She knew she had a high number of sales and had already been awarded a bestseller tag on her main sales sites, but that wasn't odd for her. She had spent the last three months avoiding reading reviews and social media, allowing Aaliyah to monitor things while she spent time with her kids. Also, criticism was hard to take right now, and this was a particularly personal story.

"Yeah! Your novel is all over the place, my girl! They even picked it up in your favorite bookstore."

"No!"

"Yes! I did a little research, and your 'dumb writing exercise' has been reviewed by the top book gurus, recommended on all the sites, and this will sound crazy, but it's in my hometown library by outrageous request and it's not the only library around here."

Annie stared as Aaliyah turned her phone to show her the computer screen. Annie had wonderful success with her books, but never to this level.

"Annie, your book is reaching debut author superstardom."

Chapter 16

Scott stepped out of the shower, drying off and wrapping the towel around his waist. He analyzed the length of his beard, the shine of his teeth, the state of his skin, and any other details to make sure they were perfect. Elizabeth was coming over for a date night, and he was feeling pretty darn good.

"She might be the one!" he said to his reflection. He rubbed his hair dry with his towel before smoothing it down with a little gel and getting dressed, taking the same care that he did with everything else. The goal—don't look like an idiot.

Over the last two months, their relationship had blossomed. Their weekly dates were all he looked forward to. It was a slight shame that her master's classes and loads of homework kept her busy most of the time, but she assured him that would change in December and then, who knew?

He had been doing his own research as well. Egypt, he found, was a fascinating country, and not just in ancient times. The findings in the latest excavations were incredibly interesting. He watched documentary after documentary to learn all he could. At first it had been to impress her, but soon it turned into his own independent interest to the point where he considered taking a trip there himself, perhaps seeing if he could persuade her to find a way to involve him on their team, maybe as the lowly water boy or unpaid pretend intern. He had a ton of savings, and a few months in Egypt wouldn't dent it at all. Of course, he wouldn't bring it up until he was confident they really liked each other and they both wanted that type of relationship. The last thing he needed was to come off as some creepy guy willing to stalk her all over the world.

When she knocked on the door, he rushed to answer it, opening the door slower than he wanted so as not to seem too eager.

"Hi, Scott," Elizabeth said brightly as she walked in, a couple of books clutched in her hands. "Mmm, what's that smell?"

"I cooked dinner," he said proudly.

"Oh, my!" she said, giving him a playful grin. "And to what do I owe this pleasure?"

"It's repayment for keeping me company. I was thinking we could have a nice homemade dinner, then cuddle and watch a movie."

"Cuddle, you say? I like that sound of that. Do you have a movie picked out?" She set her books down on the couch, then she removed her jacket and hung it familiarly on a hook next to the door.

"No, I was thinking you could help me pick."

"In that case, may I offer a different idea?" she asked. "I haven't been able to read for fun in a long time, and one of my friends insisted that I have to read this new novel. Would you mind if we cuddle and read at the same time?"

Clearly, her definition of cuddle was not the same as his. "And what will I do, admire your beauty while you read? Maybe you should sit by the window like a Regency painting and I'll draw you while you read."

"Oh, but I left my bonnet at home," she said, flipping her hair.

"You don't wear bonnets indoors, so we're good," he replied.

"Yeah, keep dreaming." She laughed. "Actually, I picked up a book at the library for you. It's about Egypt and photography. I thought it might pique your interest."

Elizabeth grabbed the book from the couch and handed it to him. He flipped through it, appreciating the mixture of text and colored photographs.

"You've won me over," he said. "Cuddle and a book it is."

They ate his dinner of spaghetti in the comfort of his dining room. He was glad he had purchased a new table and not kept the one on which his buddies had drunkenly carved "Scott is a hot stud." All his plates matched and weren't made of plastic, so he had to congratulate himself on a sophisticated meal, as sophisticated as a jar of spaghetti sauce could be.

"So, I know what my book is. What's yours?" he said

as he sat on the couch, leaning back and tapping the spot next to him.

"Mine," she said as she sat down, letting her shoes slip off her feet as she pulled her legs under her and leaned back against his shoulder, "is the next passionate romance novel."

"Really?" he snorted. "A sophisticated anthropologist reading a cheap romance novel?"

"Hey, I can read whatever I want," she said, smacking his leg. "As it happens, my best friend, Karen, passed it to me and said she cried all night over it."

"Oh, a sappy romance."

"Actually, it's supposed to be quite thoughtful, and apparently, there's a lot of speculation about it."

"How so?"

"Something about the author having a secret message or something. Karen wants me to read it so we can talk for hours dissecting it."

"Well, color me intrigued. I'll let you know if there are any discoveries as interesting in my book."

She laughed as she snuggled into him, getting comfortable as she opened her novel.

"It's called *He Will Never Know*."

"My, how captivating," he mumbled as he opened his book and read.

It was actually quite nice, nicer than he had expected. Sure, maybe he had anticipated a little romance while watching a movie they were ignoring, but he had to admit that sitting in the quiet living room, being casually close, and reading a book she had picked especially for him was special. He liked it quite a lot and could envision many nights of pleasurable reading rather than having a movie blaring and stuffing his face with popcorn.

"Aww," Elizabeth suddenly sighed.

"Oh, no," he groaned. "I'm not going to hear that all night, am I?"

"The male lead has your name."

"What a coincidence. Does the female lead have the same name as you?"

She snorted. "No. It's Annie. She was dumped by her husband, Charles, and is now dreaming about Scott."

He choked on his spit as he gasped, jumping off the couch—which almost tossed Elizabeth to the floor—and running to the bathroom. The water he chugged helped to clear his throat, and he wiped his face with a towel. He had misheard her, or it was some crazy coincidence.

He returned to the living room, feeling his face grow warm. So much for not looking like an idiot. "I'm sorry about that."

"Are you okay?" she asked. "I mean, being dumped by a husband is pretty typical in romance novels. You don't have to choke over it."

He chuckled. "No, I just swallowed wrong, and I can't have you see me so vulnerable."

"Are you afraid I'd take advantage of you?" she said with a giggle.

"I mean, if you feel so inclined," he offered, sitting back in his spot and picking up his book.

"I might after this next chapter."

"Mm-hmm. You're one of *those* girls."

"You can buy me one of those addicted mugs, the ones that say 'I can stop when I'm done with the book.'" She laughed.

"Maybe I will."

They grew silent again, and he perused the pages, taking more time to analyze the photography than read the text. It was also hard to focus with such a cute girl leaning against him, her hair smelling of strawberries and cream shampoo.

"Hmm, I didn't know this book happens in Gloucester," she mumbled. "Maybe that's why she gave it to me."

"Gloucester, Massachusetts?" he asked.

"No, Gloucester, Virginia. I mean, what writer is going to write about a romance in this Podunk town? Hey!"

At this, Scott snatched the book from her hands, looking over the cover. It was a typical modern romance cover, a little more sophisticated that a Fabio painting, but nothing out of the ordinary. The author had a name that sounded familiar, but he didn't immediately recognize it.

"What are you doing?" she asked with a laugh. "I'm reading that. I'll stop talking about it, okay?"

"Just give me a second," he said as he opened the book so he could read the description on the book flap. "'When author Annie Hayes is left by her cheating husband, a dream rekindles her feelings for an old friend, a romance that never bloomed. Wishing she could start again, she writes a novel about their time together, ending it with the romance she imagined they could have if they met again. But when her old spark discovers her novel, things get a little crazier than she intended. Will she get a second chance at love, or will her novel bring her shame?'"

"Cute, right?" Elizabeth said. "Can I have it back now?"

"Yeah," he said, passing it back. "What an interesting idea."

Elizabeth returned to her reading and Scott pretended to read his book, but his thoughts were far from it. What were the chances that a novel placed in Gloucester, Virginia—a no-account town on the York River—would have three main characters with the same first names of his past love triangle? It was uncanny. But he didn't know a Catherine Linton.

He turned another page of the photography book, staring at the carpet, his thoughts spinning round and round in a cycle of confusion. He slid his phone out of his pocket, unlocking it and typing the name *Catherine Linton* in the search bar. He sighed as the entire search page, starting with the Wiki page, only covered *Wuthering Heights* and its lead character, Catherine Linton. A memory stirred. No, it couldn't be. There had to be another explanation.

"What other books has this author written?" he asked after the space of thirty minutes.

"Hmm? Oh, I think this is her debut novel."

"That explains the lack of information about her," he mumbled.

She glanced up to see his phone in hand and huffed,

clearly amused by his interest. "Yeah, but I think it's a pen name."

"Pen name?"

"Of course," she said, closing the book, but keeping a finger firmly in the pages to save her place. "That's pretty typical for romance writers. They don't want their moms reading their work, right?" She laughed. "But I suspect this writer chose her name from that old Gothic novel, what's it called . . . *Wuthering Heights*."

"Why do you say that?" he asked.

"She's used that novel as a romance tool in this one. So she might very well have written other books under a different name, but it just as easily could be her first and she's hiding her true identity."

"Huh," he said. "Anything interesting happen so far?"

"Getting bored?" she asked. "We can do something else."

"No, I like being here with you. Tell me about what you've read. I enjoy hearing stories. I get the information without the work."

"Ha ha. Okay, my lazy man." She shifted in the seat. "Well, I like the structure she uses. She shares her history with this guy. He's a Marine with short blond hair and striking blue eyes . . . Huh, wow. That is a lot like you. And he has the same name and lives in the same town? That's unbelievable! Where does this writer live?" She flipped to the back of the book. "That's weird. Usually there's a picture with the bio. Oh, Arizona. That's pretty far. Maybe she just picked a small town with lots of bases nearby to fit the Marine backstory, but the details are uncanny."

Scott was getting nervous. "I'm sure blond, blued-eyed Marines aren't hard to come by in romance novels, and Scott isn't a rare name. So, what romantic things happen to this guy?"

She covered her face with hands for a moment as if she was going to explode before she cried out, "Oh, my goodness, Scott, he's such a cute character! They meet for a moment at a Homecoming dance where he threatens to dance with her if he sees her alone again, and then he skips class to join her art class, and then he gives her a yellow rose on Valentine's Day, claiming it's the color of friendship all because he doesn't feel good enough to court her, but he really wants to!"

Scott felt the blood drain from his face. What were the chances? It couldn't be real, but there it was in print. She had described to him all the key events from his high school romance with Annie. Or failed romance.

He got up, pretending to stretch so he could pace to get his anxious energy out. What else had that author written in that book?

"Are you okay?" Elizabeth asked, standing as she tossed the novel onto the couch. "You look sick."

"I'm actually not feeling well," he said, reaching for an excuse to cut this date short. He rubbed his stomach and stooped over slightly. "Maybe it was something I ate."

She looked concerned. "I feel fine, and I ate the same thing. Did you feel sick earlier?"

"Now that you mention it, I was feeling a little iffy

before you came. I think you should head home. I'm going to get an early night and see if that helps."

"Are you sure?" she asked as she wrapped her arms around him. "I don't want to leave you if you're sick."

"Yes, I'll be fine tomorrow. Why don't you go home and finish that novel, then tell me about it tomorrow? I'm kind of intrigued about what happens to me."

She laughed. "Maybe you should read it."

"No, thank you," he said. "I don't read romance novels. I just want the notes."

Chapter 17

Annie was standing in front of the mirror, wearing the outfit Aaliyah had picked out for her. Aaliyah wasn't her publicist, marketing team, or life coach. She was her professional editor and friend. But when Annie had been interviewed by some magazine she had never read, then asked to take a tour to twelve big bookstores in major cities around the United States, Aaliyah jumped in, insisting to go on this crazy ride with her. She was the editor of this bestselling novel, after all, and she wasn't going to let this author show up in sweats and ruin her good name. Annie usually did most of the work herself, so it had been a refreshing change to have someone else doing all the planning, and to have her own personal stylist.

Annie couldn't believe how she looked. She was self-conscious that she wasn't as small as her younger self, being a little rounder in the middle than she liked, but she had to admit that for giving birth to two kids and having gone through a divorce, she didn't look too bad.

Her waist had always been small compared to her hips,

and . . . well, her bust had never been on the small side, one reason why she had covered herself up so much in high school. Those were the features Aaliyah had pulled on to pick her outfit, and she had convinced Annie to slip into a beautifully professional and chic dress suit. The white-collared shirt was rolled at the sleeves, giving her an aura of casualness that made her feel more approachable. Her vest was tailored to pull in at her waist, the bottom edge sitting at her hip and leading the eye into the black pencil skirt that hugged her legs and stopped at her knee. She felt a little self-conscious. Her skin was still pale, seeing as she avoided the Arizona sun like the plague with the help of an umbrella and overlarge hat, but Aaliyah had assured her that newly shaved legs with the lotion she had given her and a little makeup on her face would work wonders.

"I don't know if it's me . . ." Annie mumbled.

"Honey, sweatpants and T-shirts are not book-signing appropriate," Aaliyah said as she scrolled on her phone. "Besides, you are a bestselling author now, and you know that look will not cut it outside of your house. Even if it could, I wouldn't let you. Now that we're doing a tour, Sugar, you're going to go out with your head held high and hips swinging like you're twenty-two."

"I am most definitely not twenty-two." Annie laughed, making a slight turn in the mirror. Still, she wasn't half bad for a mom hitting thirty. "It will be freezing by the time we reach Virginia."

"Bring a coat. You'll be inside most of the time. And

you are single and looking for Mr. Right," Aaliyah said. "You're a fox on the hunt."

At this, Annie scoffed so loud that Aaliyah looked up from her phone, where Annie noticed she was shopping for shoes.

"What's so funny?" Aaliyah asked. "You are, aren't you?"

"No, I'm not," Annie said. "I've only just started feeling comfortable in my own skin. Let me be single for a while, and I don't mean single and looking."

"Come on. This is the time to get out there! You'll be all over the country."

"Living out of a suitcase in cheap hotels!" Annie said in exasperation. There was no way she was going to look that good by the end of the tour. "Besides, I don't plan on remarrying."

"What? Sugar, you've still got some life in you! You don't want to spend it alone."

Annie folded her arms in defiance. "Would you say that if Marco was gone?"

"Oh, if anything happened to Marco, bless his heart, I would go out as soon as I was able. I don't believe in living in my sorrow."

"I don't live in my sorrow! And how would Marco feel knowing you would do that?"

"Oh, please! We've already talked about it, and I told him if anything happens to me, he'd better not sit on the couch eating those potato chips I won't let him have because I don't want to be living in heaven with some fat man because I wasn't there to set him straight. You know ghosts stay the same weight as when you die—"

"Oh, Aaliyah, they do not!" Annie laughed.

"Yeah, they do! Haven't you seen any movies? Poor Fantine didn't even get her hair back! Most of the time they're stuck in the same clothes, too, so you better hope you die in this outfit because those sweats do nothing for you." She pointed to the pile of clothes Annie had been wearing. "I don't think you should ever put those clothes back on. Imagine haunting your Heathcliff in that and not a dress that makes him say 'Dang, girl, you keep haunting me!'"

Annie snorted a laugh.

"Also, if Marco's going to remarry and there's any chance that I have to live with the other woman in heaven, he'd better find a good one and not some lunatic he picked up at the first bar he went to. He'd better grab some classy girl."

"This conversation just turned weird," Annie said sarcastically, turning back to the mirror and trying not to break down with laughter. Maybe she should write a new book about that.

"Besides, your ex isn't dead!" Aaliyah continued, ignoring Annie. "Charles is alive and living with his mistress-turned-wife. You can move on and find yourself a quality piece of meat who doesn't eat those stupid potato chips that blow him up like a balloon, and don't get me started on the body odor."

"I can't believe this is your motivational speech."

"Well, I'll be honest with you. I'm hoping Mr. I-wrote-him-a-love-letter-so-long-it's-a-bestselling-novel shows up, and if that happens, I want you to look so smokin' hot, he won't be able to resist sweeping you off your feet!"

Heat rose to Annie's face and she felt a wave of nausea. "You don't think that's possible, do you?"

Aaliyah gave her a sly smile, then peered back at her phone. "All things are possible with God and Aaliyah."

"But we used a pen name to make sure he wouldn't ever read it or figure it out."

"We didn't change the location and their first names," Aaliyah said under her breath, still smiling as she swiped on her phone. "What ridiculous Cinderella-sized shoe are you again?"

"Did you trick me?" Annie hissed. "Did you give me poor advice that I followed because I assumed my sassy friend would look out for me?"

"Or good advice. Only time will tell. Does your friend read romance novels?"

"No! I don't know. Probably not."

"Then it's not a problem. Just my wish as your fairy godmother. Now, what was that shoe size?"

Annie rolled her eyes. "If you're going to buy shoes, make sure they're flats and not heels. I have too much walking to do, and I don't care how good heels make my butt look."

"Okay, I promise. Size?"

"And they probably won't fit, and I hate sending stuff back."

Aaliyah waved her hand in dismissal. "Please, I send so much stuff back, the UPS guy and I are on a first-name basis."

"And please make them black, nothing flashy."

"Any more requests, Your Majesty?" Aaliyah snapped.

"Four and a half wide."

Chapter 18

Scott's phone was turned off and under his pillow while he took a rake to the frozen leaf pile that was his front yard. That way, he would stop wondering if he heard his phone ring and have to focus on his busy work. Elizabeth wouldn't call until she was done with her paper, which wasn't usually until six p.m. Until then, he would have to wait and pour all his nerves, curiosity, confusion, and honestly, his budding anger into the miles of leaves and branches blanketing his front yard.

Catherine Linton, whoever she was, had too much information about him. Though Elizabeth could shrug it off as a weird coincidence, he knew better. Of course, there could be more than one blue-eyed, blond-haired Marine named Scott who grew up in Gloucester, Virginia, but not one who had met a girl at a Homecoming dance only to spend his time skipping classes to spend art class with her, and then give her a yellow rose on Valentine's Day. And it was clear that *Wuthering Heights* was an important book to this author. Or at least, to the person who had all this information.

He wondered if it could be a sick joke. He couldn't imagine the novel would end well for him, given what happened between them. He had not been kind, but a broken heart was prone to doing ridiculous and uncharacteristic things. It was *broken*, after all! He knew that his character would inevitably turn into the villain, and that was defamation of character. He wasn't able to defend himself, and it would only be a matter of time before it got out that he *was* the villain and that the story she wrote was based on truth.

Six p.m. couldn't come fast enough. He hoped Elizabeth had spent the entire night reading that stupid book so she could confirm his suspicions. Maybe he should have just read it himself, but the anger he already felt rising made him unsure if he could handle reading it. Taking a deep breath and letting Elizabeth give him the synopsis was better. He didn't need more demons rising.

He was pacing the living room floor with a freshly charged and turned on phone at exactly six p.m.

"Hey there, handsome," she said when she called ten minutes later.

"Hey, how is it going?" he replied, trying to sound normal.

"Are you feeling better?"

"Yes," he said, taking a step outside and sitting in a chair he had set up on the porch. "Did you get much reading done?"

"Yeah, I'm about halfway through, but then my professor called and had me fill out some interview questions for the excavation. But I plan on finishing it tonight if I can."

"Is it good?"

"Yeah, it's been great so far, but man, the Scott character—"

"What about him?"

"I just feel bad for him. He gets all bitter and angry because she falls for someone else, and he does some not-nice things."

"Typical romance stuff, huh?" he interrupted, his fears confirmed.

"Yeah." She laughed. "But you'll never guess what Karen told me today."

"I'm sure I couldn't," he joked.

"She said the author, Catherine Linton, is doing a book signing in Richmond this weekend! What are the chances? I know you're not interested in romance novels, but I like her style and I really want to meet her. Would you like to go with me? It's at the store off Broad Street near Monument Avenue. I thought we could grab some dinner and take a pleasant stroll down Cary Street. What do you think?"

Scott couldn't believe his luck. He could confront this author, figure out how she knew so much, and have a nice date with Elizabeth. It seemed like a good deal all around.

"I think that sounds great."

With his hair perfect and clothes specially chosen to look smart and professional, he hoped to put fear and regret into the heart of this author while still making Elizabeth glad he was with her.

"This is really exciting," Elizabeth said from the passenger seat, clutching the book in her hands. "I'll have to buy my own copy. Karen couldn't make it, so she asked me to get it signed for her."

"I'm sure there will be plenty of copies. Did you ever finish it?"

"Oh, yes. It was heartbreaking and wonderful."

"I bet."

"I know you aren't into romance novels. I'm not usually either, but I'm really intrigued by this one."

"How so?"

"Well, Catherine Linton did an interview where she was asked if she wrote the book for someone, like some sort of layered *Inception*-type thing. Did she write this novel as a love letter to someone in real life? If so, it's a writer writing a love letter novel to an old flame about a writer who's writing a book to an old flame. It's really cool."

Scott looked at Elizabeth. "And what did she say?"

"The interviewer said she put on a coy smile and replied, 'Wouldn't that be interesting?' and left it at that! She sounds like a character."

He huffed. "I guess we'll see."

The bookstore was packed when they arrived, and Elizabeth quickly purchased a copy of the book and joined the other enthusiastic romance readers in line. There were too many people to get a good look at the author, though Scott could tell she had short dark hair and wore glasses. Elizabeth chatted happily next to him, and he smiled and grunted as necessary, preoccupied with how he was going to tell this author off. Should he make a big scene and threaten to sue her? Should he lean in and whisper that he was coming after her and would see her in court, then revel in the shock on her face? That would probably be better, for Elizabeth's sake.

As they grew closer to the table, only three people back, he could finally get a good look at her face, and he froze. Her hair was short now, not long and tied in a ponytail. Her face was bright and confident as she took the book from the next person, smiling widely, her lips a glossy bold red, her eyes looking large with the cat-eye liner accenting them. As she spoke to her fans, not a hint of the timidity she had worn in high school showed through. Of course, her face had aged slightly, her cheeks were more defined, and that crease between her eyes appeared to be permanent. She was also chubbier, but not incredibly so. More like the weight one naturally puts on as they age. Overall, he couldn't fault her looks, which would have made what he had to do easier.

Chapter 19

Annie was having a wonderful time. This was the last stop on their tour, and by now, she was a pro. She had never met so many fans face-to-face before. All her previous book signings had been one-offs with very few people, not huge lines in some of the biggest bookstores around, and in multiple cities to boot! Even the August book signing in Phoenix, which she had planned herself, had been tiny. She loved hearing people's stories and how her novel had affected them. There had been a few occasions where tears were shed by both parties as confessions of cheating husbands and divorces were shared, and women said her book had given them hope for a better future.

There were also the people who wanted selfies with her, those who weren't sure who she was, but had a sister who read books so it was convenient to get it signed, and of course, those who earnestly, desperately wanted to know the truth—was this novel actually a love letter?

She had made sure to keep it vague. She didn't want to lie because it was, in fact, true. She had written a love letter. She had poured out all her pain, confessed all her views and faults, and tried to explain why she had done what she did. Then, in her own way, she had asked for him back, giving him an enticing taste of how it could be.

Of course, she knew it was all for naught, but why tell her fans that? Why not have this tantalizing secret that people could speculate about? It was great publicity, and perfect gossip for the romance reader. So she kept them guessing, giving them winks and vague responses to the questions of why she wrote the book. She had convinced herself that there was no harm done, and she quelled the fears she had of Scott finding out and coming after her for legal reasons.

So when she looked up at the book signing in Richmond and saw Scott's glowering face only three people away with a girl hanging on his arm and chatting happily at him, her fight-or-flight response kicked in and she stood up, yelling, "Restroom break! Excuse me!" and made a dash for the exit, which was not the restroom. Thank goodness Aaliyah had bought her flats.

"Hey!" Aaliyah yelled. She had been grazing at a bookshelf nearby and threw down the book she was reading to take off after Annie.

Annie was fumbling with the keys to her car when Aaliyah caught up, snatching them from her hand with an angry, "What in the world do you think you're doing? What is the matter?"

"He's here," she stammered through her hyperventilating lungs, puffs of cold air billowing from her trembling lips. "He's here."

"Who's here?" Aaliyah asked.

"Scott."

"How do you—?"

But it was too late. Before Aaliyah could finish her sentence, Scott's voice reached them from across the parking lot, followed swiftly by him and a poor girl running to keep up, two books clutched in her arms. "Where do you think you're going, Annie?"

She clawed at the handle of her car, but it was still locked, the keys hanging from Aaliyah's fingers. Why did he have to look so handsome? Why did he have to show up like this, his voice fuming rather than soft and loving like in her book? Why did it have to happen like this? If she couldn't flee, Annie decided, she would have to fight. She held up her chin, took a deep breath, and turned around, putting her hands on her hips. He had never seen her in makeup, a dress, and shoes that fit before, and obviously ten years older. Maybe if she played it right, she could convince him she was someone else. Catherine Linton, perhaps.

"Can I help you, sir?" she said, her body trembling. She hoped it looked like she was shivering from the late autumn air and not nerves.

"Don't *sir* me, missy," he scolded. "You know why I'm here."

She raised her eyebrows, feigning surprise as she smiled widely. "Of course. You want me to sign your books." She took them from Elizabeth, who looked between the two with growing confusion as Annie leaned against the car and opened the book covers.

"Do you have a pen, Aaliyah? I left mine at the table." She forced her voice to be light, trying to sound conversational rather than panicky. "I had an emergency come up, but you must be desperate for my signature, so I can spare a moment."

Aaliyah caught on to her ploy, pulling out a pen and handing it to her. "Of course, Catherine," she said, emphasizing her name and turning to Elizabeth. "Who should Mrs. Linton make it out to?"

"This one's for Karen, and this is mine, Elizabeth," Elizabeth said, indicating between the two.

"Wonderful!" Annie scribbled her usual message, struggling to keep the pen steady as her hand shook.

"Don't act like you don't know me, Annie," Scott said, moving beside her and getting close enough that she could smell his cologne, the same he had worn in high school. "You had no right to make this book."

"I'm not—" she tried to insist as her heart pounded both from fear and his presence, but he glared at her.

"Do you think it's a joke, sharing all that stuff about me with the world? Did you think to make riches off embarrassing me?"

Annie dropped the act, finishing the note swiftly as she turned to face him. "It's you who seems to think my book is a joke," she snapped. "How dare you come up to me like this instead of talking to me like a decent human being."

"Oh, don't turn this around on me. Did you think I wouldn't find out? You didn't even bother to change our names or the location. And now you act like it's no big deal!"

"Oh, my gosh, you really are Annie?" Elizabeth said, her smile widening as she took the books that Annie had robotically given her. "I'm so . . . Is this book really about Scott?"

Both of them turned to Elizabeth, and Annie felt sick at the sight of the beautiful young woman, wrapped elegantly in a form fitting coat and tucked scarf.

"I'm sorry that we haven't been properly introduced," Annie said. "I'm Annie Allred, also known as Catherine Linton, which is a secret," she hissed in a whisper as she glanced accusingly at Scott. "And you must be Scott's wife." This she said in a much nicer, though strained, voice.

Elizabeth gave an awkward laugh. "No, I'm just his girlfriend."

"Oh," Annie said, her surprise showing, before she added, "Has he changed much?" She pointed to the book.

"That's it!" Scott shouted. "Annie, I'm coming after you for libel and defamation of character. You can't do this! There are laws."

"It can't be libel if it's true," Annie replied.

"She's right, Scott. If what she wrote is true, even if you don't like it, you don't have a case there," Elizabeth agreed.

"And it's not defamation of character!" Annie

continued, emboldened by Elizabeth's support. "If I were going to do that, I wouldn't have written a romance! Or I would have made you a far less attractive character, which I am starting to regret. Defamation, indeed. It's like you didn't even read the book."

Elizabeth eyed Scott, giving him a guilty stare, and for a moment, Scott looked dumbfounded.

Annie was appalled. "You didn't read the book? You have the gall to threaten me with lawsuits when you haven't even read the book in question? Scott, you are unbelievable!"

She took a deep breath and tried to stop the tears that were welling up in her eyes. She hoped her makeup was magically waterproof because the last thing she wanted to do was look awful in front of stupid Scott and his stupid girlfriend with all her fans watching this stupid argument from the stupid bookstore. She was certain she saw somebody's smartphone reflecting light from the window and was mortified that this could all be on the booktube blogs within the hour, if it wasn't being shown live!

"That book helped me heal from my broken marriage. That book is as honest as I could make it, and even though I should have thought through the details better and maybe been smarter and not followed poor advice . . ." She glanced at Aaliyah, who gave a weak smile. "It was written with the purest and deepest . . . and . . . Gah!" She fumbled with her words, tears running down her cheeks. "You're stupid, Scott, and I'm wearing sweats for the rest of my life so that when I die, you'll be miserable. No nice dress for you!"

"Oh, sugar, that's not what I meant," Aaliyah muttered.

"Until that time, I never want to see you again. It was nice meeting you, Elizabeth. I hope he makes you very happy."

With this, she snatched the keys from Aaliyah's weakened grip and clambered into the car, started it, blasted the radio to muffle any protests already quieted by the window, and drove off in what she hoped was a dramatic exit. Might as well make it good for her fans.

Though she wanted to drive back to the hotel and bury her head under her pillow, she didn't go far, parking behind a building a couple of streets over. She took her phone out of her pocket, thankful that pockets were essential to Aaliyah because she probably would have left it on the table otherwise, and texted her editor-turned-publicist, asking her to message when Scott was gone. At that time, she would return and finish the signing. She tossed her phone on the passenger seat, slid off her glasses, and sobbed.

Chapter 20

Scott, Elizabeth, and Aaliyah stood helplessly as Annie's car skidded out of the parking lot.

"She was my ride," Aaliyah said casually, leaning down and picking up the pen Annie had dropped in her rush to get away. She pointed at Scott. "I hope she comes back. If not, I'll be sending you a bill for my cab."

"What was she talking about with the sweats?" Scott asked.

Aaliyah turned to him, cocking her hip. "Sugar, I suggest you read that book." She clicked the pen, taking Scott's hand and writing on it. "This is my number. I'm not hitting on you. I got a handsome man at home who would squash you flat. Call me when you finish reading, and then we'll talk." She clicked the pen again, then made her way back to the bookstore, shouting out assurances that the book signing would continue in a little while.

Scott stared at the number on his palm. He was feeling a mixture of shame and confusion. He realized he had come to this ill-prepared—which wasn't like him at all, stupid demons—and he wondered exactly how foolish he looked.

Elizabeth slid her hand into his and gave it a squeeze. He glanced at her, and she gave him a small smile. "Let's go. I'll drive."

He didn't argue.

She took them down Cary Street and parked the car next to the restaurant they had discussed earlier. She rebutted any argument about going home and made him sit across from her at the table of her choice.

"Now, Scott," she said. "I need you to listen to what I have to say."

"There's nothing to say," he said, covering his face with his hands. "I made a fool of myself and embarrassed you. I should have told you the truth. I thought I would handle it, intimidate the author, and we'd go on our date and I'd never give it another thought. I'm sorry."

"I'm not mad," she said, though her voice held a heaviness that Scott recognized and wasn't ready for.

He leaned across the table and grabbed her hands. "I made a mistake. Don't end our relationship over this. I'm so happy that we met, and I want to see where this goes."

She shook her head. "That's not it. If I had known the novel was based on you, I would have insisted you read it. The thing is, I'm not a fan of what-ifs. I don't believe in living life that way. I prefer to resolve things rather than leaving doubt, and I can't be with someone who doesn't. I can't continue this relationship until you've read this book and explored your what-ifs. My professor told me I made the team. I'm leaving in December to do some research at Oxford before joining the excavation in the summer. We've only been together for a few months, and though I really, really like you, I can walk away now without too much heartbreak."

"I don't have any what-ifs," he assured her. "I haven't thought about Annie in years. Really, I don't know what she wrote, but I assure you, I have no feelings for her whatsoever. It was over ten years ago, for goodness' sake!"

She squeezed his hand. "If you don't read this book now, you'll think, 'What if there's something in there I didn't know?' until you do. And when you do, you'll continue to think 'What if?' for the rest of your life. We may have a future together, but I can't live with a man who might succumb to what-ifs. So, I'm giving you space while my heart can take it. You read that book because if it were me and everything in that book is true, I would have some 'what-ifs' that I'd want to explore."

"What did she write that's such a big deal?" he asked. "Aren't I the bad guy?"

Elizabeth smiled. "Oh, Scott, not by a long shot."

Scott sat on his bed, holding the book Elizabeth had let him borrow. He cracked open the cover and saw the chicken-scratch signature of Catherine Linton. *Everyone deserves a second chance*, she had written.

He sighed, leaning back on the bed and turning the page. He didn't want to read it, feared reading it, was still angry and embarrassed, but if he wanted a relationship with Elizabeth, he had to read this book and prove that there were no what-ifs. Then he could call that lady who wrote her number on his hand and find out why Annie had been going on about sweat pants.

The first chapter was a little difficult to read. He didn't enjoy experiencing Annie's divorce, her children, or the affair. He was surprised at her honesty and a little angry at Charles. Charles had the gumption to take her from him and then threw her away like that. He felt a slight validation of his feelings for the man in the past. Charles didn't do his best to deserve her, as Scott knew he wouldn't, though he had wished otherwise.

Elizabeth had warned him, but he was still surprised to find that the entire second chapter, and those alternating, were not only about him, but from his point of view. He assumed Annie's view was accurate, but she hadn't gotten all of his viewpoint right, though she justified some motives and expressed his underlying feelings fairly well. But being a teenage boy, it wasn't that hard to figure it out. His friends and mother were fictional, and as she had never met either, that made sense. He wondered how accurate she would have been if she had. It didn't take long for him to get engrossed in the story.

Memories change over time. Scenes recede so they're seen from the outside rather than through the eyes. Words get lost, leaving only the impression, the feelings they had that are powerful enough to stay potent, and even then, will fade. Seeing the past through her eyes brought forth the memories he had repressed and dragged along the feelings with it. He didn't know how long she had cared for him. He didn't know how easily he could have won her, and how forgiving and understanding, how merciful she would have been to his lost soul.

Her confessions, which filled her chapters and even his, softened his heart, and without realizing it, his anger had faded. By chapter nine, he felt his heart pounding as she described the kiss in his car and realized he was holding his breath. When he let it out, his vision turned a little fuzzy. How he had loved her! He had forgotten, stuffed it inside, ran from it around the world, but having it thrown in his face like this brought it all back with such force, he wanted to tear his heart from his chest to stop the pain. At the time, he wasn't sure how life could get better than when she ran out to kiss him. And she was right—he had spent many a random night, even years later, wondering why she had done that, then married that idiot.

He knew what was coming, the bitter ending they would have, brief in description and accurate to the emotions—if not his memory—of events. Her point of view was logical, and he sympathized now, though he hadn't seen it that way at all. To her, this was all truth, and he couldn't fault her for her feelings.

When that chapter ended, there was still half a book left, and he expected her continuation of the love story with Charles and that would end her sad, romantic book, a memoir disguised as fiction.

But that wasn't at all what he discovered. The rest of the book *was* complete fiction, a completely made-up tale about her writing a novel that brought them back together. He realized now why he was the bad guy, not in the book, but in real life. In the novel, he had read the story and sought her out with love on his mind. In reality, he hadn't read the book, and he sought her out in anger.

He soon found the passage Elizabeth knew would touch his heart.

> Too many times, we forget people are human, that they have feelings, that they make mistakes. Too many times, we cling to our pain and refuse to see that life goes on, emotions calm down, and people regret. And she regretted and forgave and wished she could say all the things she wanted to say, but knowing it was too late and not wanting to upset his life, she wrote them, honestly and plainly, in a book. Without ever intending him to see it, she wrote him a love novel, the longest love letter she had ever written, and signed it to him under a false name, and sent it into the universe, subconsciously hoping and wishing that something would come back.

He stared at the page. Her heroine had written and published the book, just as she had. Was Annie, the real Annie, wanting Scott to come back? Was this actually a love letter for him?

A knot was forming in his throat. As angry as he had been, as frustrated and bitter and cruel as he had been, he knew he could make one of two choices. He could prove—because of her foolish mistake—that this book was about him and take her to court, sapping her money and soiling her name all because she chose Charles (a truly delicious Heathcliff thing to do), or he could forgive her, embrace the emotions that he clenched within his chest, and take the risk. He would lose his chance with Elizabeth, lose his chance at a new life, but he might get what Annie was also hoping for—a second chance.

When she wrote this story, Annie had wanted him. Would she still want him after what he'd done? And did he actually want her, or was it a fleeting emotion? He would have said no in an instant before he read the book. He *had* said no! But now . . . what if? What if he forgave the past? What if he opened his mind to her point of view, allowed her choice to be right? What if they genuinely weren't ready then, but life experience had made them ready now? What if he gave it a chance? What if she was Catherine, and he was Heathcliff? What if . . .

He looked down at the number on his palm. He supposed it was time to figure out why she had been raving about sweatpants making him miserable after her death.

Chapter 21

Annie was glad to return to Arizona, even though Arizona was not her home. She didn't really like it. It was sunny and dry, even in the winter. She didn't tan, so any time she spent in the sun was under the shade of a tree, a porch, or an umbrella. She hated being the weird umbrella lady in her new neighborhood, but she had moved to Arizona with her husband, had given birth here, and now the parenting agreement made her stay here. Even so, the miserable meeting with Scott in Virginia had squashed any desire she had to be anywhere but right here. Here she had a house, her kids, and was contemplating a puppy. Dogs loved unconditionally, even if they peed on the carpet. Her kids had peed on her couch when they were potty training, and they loved her unconditionally. Maybe a dog would bring the comfort and love she would never get from a man, and dogs could be trained to stay.

The phone in her pocket vibrated, and she switched the umbrella to her other hand so she could pull it out.

Aaliyah's face popped up as she answered it.

"Hey, what's up?" Annie asked.

"Getting some sun?" Aaliyah said, trying not to laugh.

"Trying not to, actually."

"Ah, my little tomato. Well, do you want to hear some good news?"

"After the fiasco all over my social media last week? Anything would be good."

"Oh, don't hold on to that! That was great publicity."

"Watching me and Scott argue and reveal my identity to everyone is not great publicity. I've never been more embarrassed and ashamed in my life! Now I'm the creepy girl writing fake stories about ex-boyfriends because she can't move on. Oh, my goodness, I'll never live it down!" She sniffed, fighting the tingling in her nose with a vicious rub of her wrist.

"You haven't been keeping up with the story, though! Have you checked your sales?"

"No. I haven't gone onto the computer since I saw Mikel's video post tearing me apart."

"Go check them now."

Reluctantly, Annie entered the house and turned on her computer, bringing up the website with her spreadsheets.

"What in the world . . . ?" she whispered, scrolling and refreshing the page to make sure it wasn't a mistake. "Where did all these sales come from?"

"That's what I've been saying. I've been watching all the stuff on you because I knew you wouldn't, and this infamous story has blown your book up. Everyone is loving what you did, putting your heart out there."

"Scott is going to sue the pants off me," Annie muttered. "At least I can pay the lawyer."

"You really think Scott is going to sue you?"

"After this video release? Yes!"

Aaliyah tsked. "I don't think that's going to happen. He's not that bad."

"How would you know?"

"Because I talked to him on the phone."

Annie choked. "W-when?"

"A few days ago."

"And you didn't tell me?"

"Nah, I figured I'd get around to it."

"Did he *say* he wouldn't sue me?" Annie asked. "What did you tell him?"

"I told him you were at home this weekend and that the kids were at their dad's. Oh, and I gave him your address."

"What?"

"He should be arriving about now."

"What?" Annie cried.

A knock pounded on the door, and Annie's heart stopped.

"Call me later, Sugar," Aaliyah said before the screen went blank.

Annie didn't have to answer the door. She could pretend she wasn't home, but Aaliyah was probably texting him. She knew for a fact that Annie was home. However, Annie had prepared for multiple different scenarios, and having anticipated this one—she was a romance writer, after all—she grabbed a certain worn book from the top of the bookshelf.

She checked the waist of her sweatpants, smoothed out her T-shirt, and held her head high as she walked to the door and opened it, leaning against it as casually as she could manage. She hoped.

"Ah, look what the cat dragged in," she said, trying to sound calm and placing her hand on her hip.

Scott laughed, shifting his head to the side. "Is that the outfit you're going to haunt me in?" he asked. "It's not that bad."

She licked her lips as she looked at the ground. "Aaliyah told you."

"She did," he replied.

"And what else did you talk about?"

"Mostly your book."

"Did you read it?"

"Yes, I did."

"Do you have a court date for me, or will you be sending your lawyer over to hand me the papers?" she asked. "Personally, I think I caught your character very well, especially in chapter ten, you know, where you say 'Goodbye, Mrs. Allred,' throw that book in my face, and slam the door. Well, here's my revenge, Heathcliff. Goodbye, Mr. Candon." And with that, she shoved the book into his chest, sending him a few steps backward, and slammed the door in his face, locking it.

She grabbed her phone and texted Aaliyah.

HE WILL NEVER KNOW

Annie: I love you, but if you fraternize with that stupid, heartless, bitter man after this, I will never speak to you again.

Chapter 22

Scott supposed he shouldn't be surprised that she slammed the door in his face. He hadn't been able to explain anything. Aaliyah had warned him that Annie was angry, that she had insisted all her feelings for him, the fantasy she had foolishly made, was gone. He had hoped she was exaggerating. Was Annie going to keep being this stubborn?

He knocked again, but she ignored him. He tried knocking more times, but Annie's children seemed to have imbued her with the power to ignore loud, obnoxious things without feeling the need to tell them to be quiet, and it was with great reluctance that he left her house, fearing she might call the police for harassment, and instead left to find a hotel where he could recoup.

His phone dinged.

Aaliyah: How did it go?

Scott: Not so good.

Aaliyah: Dang! I thought the good news would cheer her up enough to hear you out. What's your plan?

Scott: Find a hotel for the night.

Aaliyah: What? Prince Charming, you've got to try harder than that!

Scott: I'm not Prince Charming, I'm Heathcliff. I will, I just have to think about it.

Aaliyah: Ok. Text me if you need advice. And you will.

Scott gave an exasperated sigh. He had purchased his own copy of her book and had returned Elizabeth's shortly before he had taken a plane to Arizona. Elizabeth had held him for a long time before she said goodbye. He could text her if Annie refused to speak with him, but he knew she wasn't expecting him to. His what-if list was too long not to try everything. If Annie had been uglier, or sillier, he might have known the answer and been repulsed by her immediately, much like Charles Dickens when he became reacquainted with his first love, but she was more beautiful than he had ever seen her, and her writing showed all the wit and intelligence that had made him fall for her in the first place.

He pulled into the driveway of a hotel. Looking at the book laying on the passenger seat, the one she had shoved at him before closing the door, he chuckled. Annie was always a girl who enjoyed karma. He picked up the book. *Wuthering Heights*. He opened the cover and saw the inscription she had written to him over ten years ago. The page now had a wrinkled quality, and the ink was blurred in a few spots.

He opened his new copy of *He Will Never Know* and turned to the quote she had used from *Wuthering Heights*.

> He shall never know I love him: and that, not because he's handsome, but because he's more myself than I am. Whatever our souls are made out of, his and mine are the same.

He felt this. It resonated with him in a strange way, but there was a flaw in the statement. He now knew that she had loved him.

Pulling a pen out of his pocket, Scott opened Annie's book to the first chapter and started to cross parts out and scribble over the page. He sat there for hours, making notes, folding edges for bookmarks, writing new passages, and pointing out all that she had gotten wrong.

He suddenly realized he was not Heathcliff.

Chapter 23

Annie was a little heartsick when Scott left. She was angry—with herself, with him, with Aaliyah. She had thought it would all go differently. He was never supposed to read the book—or, as fairy godmother Aaliyah had wished, he was supposed to read the book and come for her, make some romantic gesture similar to what she had written. But that's not what she got. She couldn't handle more time in the courtroom. She couldn't cope with dragging her kids through this drama. She would have to pull the book, the most successful novel she had ever written, the longest love letter in the history of love letters, and pay all the money it had received to Scott, who would use it to marry his beautiful Elizabeth and live happily ever after. And she would adopt a puppy and possibly never write again.

The next day brought another knock on her door. She answered it, expecting to find Scott. Her mouth was open, prepared with another rebuttal, but she snapped it shut. It was not Scott. Though the man held an air of familiarity, he was a stranger to her. He ran his hand down his groomed beard as he asked, "Catherine Linton?"

"Yes?" she said.

"Good day. My name is Mr. Dean. I have here a package from one Scott Candon with evidence that is to be reviewed by Catherine Linton before her court date—today the twelfth of November at 12:15 p.m." He held out a thick manila envelope, a yellow sticky note with the date, times, and location of the court on the front.

"What?" she asked, hardly sure what she was hearing.

"You are being served, and this is your summons. He's suing you on counts of libel and a right of privacy violation. I highly recommend reviewing the evidence swiftly. He has made his case quite well, and I doubt you will win."

"I-I don't have time to get a lawyer!" she replied. "They don't assign court dates this quickly. You must have the wrong day."

"I assure you, I do not. I confirmed the times with the courts just ten minutes ago."

"This is absurd. Don't I have the right for more time? This has to be illegal."

"I'm afraid this is a particularly poignant case, and the judge was very keen to resolve it. You'll be assigned a lawyer if you don't have one." He glanced casually at his watch. "Officers will arrive at noon to make sure you attend."

"What?"

"This is a very serious matter, Mrs. Linton. I'm sorry to bring you this news, but I recommend you review the evidence immediately and pray the judge is lenient."

She had thought he might try to sue her, but she didn't think it happened like this. However, she'd never been sued before. She tried to recall any legal research she had done for her books, but her mind was blank, spinning in circles as she tried to comprehend what was happening. She snatched the manila folder from him and slammed the door before he could say, "Have a nice day."

She picked up the phone, struggling to call Aaliyah with hands shaking so badly, she could hardly see them.

"What's up, sugar?"

"Scott's suing me!" she yelled. "For libel and invasion of privacy or something."

"What?" Aaliyah cried. "Okay, calm down. When's the court date?"

"Today! And they're sending police to my house to escort me. That doesn't sound right to me at all."

"Oh, dang, they only do that for serious cases. It happened to my cousin! They came and got him, sentenced him, and put him in prison the same day!"

"I'm not a criminal!" Annie said. "This is ridiculous!"

"Don't panic!" Aaliyah said, her voice shaking. "Did they give you any evidence to review?"

"Yes." Tears streamed down Annie's cheeks. "They gave me an envelope."

"That's good! I know it's going to be hard, but I need you to calm down and focus. I'm going to head over there. You read what they gave you, and I'll help you make a case before the police get there."

"They'll be here at noon."

"Okay, I'm on my way. Read the evidence."

Aaliyah hung up, and Annie dropped the phone. What about her girls? What would this do to them? She'd have to call Charles and tell him everything. Her gut twisted. She would do that later, maybe with her one phone call. She only had two hours to prepare.

She took a deep breath, sitting at her desk and opening the envelope. She slid out a book and immediately recognized a copy of her novel. Strips of white paper stuck out like bookmarks, and the book was expanded from all the dog ears. She opened it to the first page and saw a note.

> Annie,
>
> I have taken great care to mark all the passages that are incorrect, and therefore libel. Seeing as I and others could recognize this character as me, I will require monetary compensation for a violation of my rights to privacy. Please review the notes and be prepared.
>
> Scott

That stupid, vengeful, conceited, prideful, unforgiving man!

Annie turned to the first chapter and found a few

markings there, not unlike the way he had done with their copy of *Wuthering Heights*. She flipped to the next chapter and saw words scribbled out and notes written in. Had he edited and commented on her entire book? This was ridiculous. She couldn't possibly read through all these notes in two hours. She picked up a red pen from her desk and made her plan—she would strike out anything that was a weak argument and focus only on the things she thought could be defended in a proper court.

This proved immensely helpful since the first few pages only contained terse notes such as "My eyes are sapphire, not blue. Please be more accurate," "The Homecoming dance music was really more hip hop than rap," and "I am a Marine! I am an exquisite cleaner. My home is spotless." A quick swipe and she moved on.

But when she found this note in chapter four, she wasn't at all sure what to think and almost forgot that she was supposed to be making a case for court.

> Here you state I fell in love with you as we sat outside talking on the baseball field. That is far from true, and the worst libel yet. Missy, I fell in love with you the moment you looked up at me with those 'large, hazel eyes.' Do you think I threaten to dance with strangers all the time? And to hip hop?

She flipped the page, swiping through what had to be

snide jokes made to throw her off, searching for more. In chapter five, she found a paragraph circled with an adjacent comment written on a strip of paper.

> She suddenly became acutely aware that she was still dressed in her gym uniform—black shorts and a red shirt, covered by her dependable hooded sweater with the holes in the sleeves—and terribly, embarrassingly sweaty, a combination of too much running and Virginia humidity. She wished beyond all wishes that she was wearing anything else.

Here you suggest you are a hot mess and that I comment you are cute. I would like to clarify that this is false. You were not at all a hot mess. As I recall, and I'm sure my memory is as good as yours, it was the first time that I could see how truly feminine you were. Your eyes were bright and your cheeks were flushed, but there were no signs of dripping sweat. And the shape of your legs! Being the first time I had ever seen so much of your skin, even though other girls showed that area all the time, I felt like I was being ungentlemanly! And when I offered the rose, which I declared was for friendship, I was sure you had seen past me and knew that I cared.

Annie was surprised that she laughed. She stopped. This wasn't right. Wasn't he suing her? Was this written in anger or with affection? She could hardly tell. She turned the page, looking for more and finding another in the same chapter from when she gave him the copy of *Wuthering Heights*.

> "Look, missy, if I didn't like it, I would tell you. Yes, I'm that mean. I love it, Annie. Thanks."
>
> She nodded, hoping he didn't notice the tears she was fighting back—tears of relief.

The clear fact is, I did notice the tears, and I panicked, thinking I had hurt your feelings. I wanted to hold you and apologize, but I couldn't. I didn't know how you would react to that, so instead, I casually talked about anything else. You didn't notice how tightly I held on to the book. No one had ever given me such a nice gift, and I hoped beyond hope that it meant you might possibly care for me.

She turned eagerly to chapter six and read a comment about when she was playing the piano for him.

> Her hands returned to the keys and started playing a song in stark contrast to the last. It was slow and soulful, almost like a ballad, and Scott couldn't stop himself from reaching

out and laying a hand on her shoulder. She jumped lightly, but didn't falter.

Suddenly her brother Allen walked into the room, and she sprang from the piano.

Ignoring your terrible speculation on my childhood in this chapter, I'm disappointed that you omitted such a crucial fact and an event so terribly misrepresented! I had asked permission, if you recall, to braid your hair while you played, and you gave your consent. How could you not elaborate on the softness of your hair in my fingers as I twisted the braid together? How could you not envision the pleasure I felt at being able to stand behind you as you played, creating such a heavenly intimate scene, so much that on having someone see us, you sprang from the piano, such the innocent lamb that you were? I didn't doubt that you were embarrassed by your brother's approach, and I longed to tell you I loved you, and only my desire to be close to you had pushed me to touch your shoulder as you played. For shame.

And just below, it read,

That was the second time he had touched her that day, and he gave himself a mental high five. He was on his way.

This is actually exceedingly true.

She had remembered him braiding her hair and had left it out on purpose. It had felt too intimate to share, though she saw now how innocent it was. But she had felt the heat from his touch and had run at the first opportunity, hoping to spare his feelings, because she hadn't known what to do, how to interpret its meaning, and was unsure of what to say. It had seemed best to avoid it altogether.

Then she found chapter eight.

> Was she some constant, impervious angel, some figment from God sent to torture him for his misbehavior?

I cannot tell you how many times I asked this question! How could one person be so unchangeable in attitude, looks, and beliefs? There was no rebelling, no drastic change to prove you had reached adulthood. What happened to make you so true? And how did I, this fluctuating, inconstant wretch, get to be friends with you? Why did you give me attention? Why hadn't you shunned me like so many others? Why had you made me feel worthwhile? Yes, why had you been sent to torture me? To gaze at me with those eyes and make me want you so much? Did I have any hope of reaching you or having you for myself?

She was instantly hit with such a sense of longing, the old feelings she had for Scott rising within her. Hadn't she felt all those things? Hadn't she wondered why he never cared for her? Why he would show up in her life then disappear as though he didn't care, but then do something so tender and wonderful that she *felt* all the things he wanted to say, but didn't realize it? Why couldn't she have been as she was now? She was older and wiser—she would have seen it today.

The heat rose in her face as she suddenly remembered chapter ten, the chapter of passion and heartache. What had he made of those chapters?

She swiped at the pages, almost tearing them in her eagerness to read his notes.

> The first kiss, he could have dismissed. But it was the second kiss, the kiss that she didn't need to give him, the kiss that had made him lose his mind for a moment, and only a stupid seat belt and car door had stopped him from acting on it.

This is outrageously inaccurate, and frankly, I'm appalled by your lack of imagination and description. That kiss sent electricity through me, and my heart was close to stopping. That kiss, the kiss that I knew was freely given, was the kiss I had been longing for since I met you. It was the Golden Fleece, the Holy Grail, the unobtainable object that had somehow willingly come to me. At that point, I was convinced beyond a doubt that I had finally won you, and it was only a matter of time before I could whisk you away and share my life with you.

There was a note in bold letters that read *skip to the red pen in chapter eleven*. She suddenly remembered she was supposed to be making notes for a defense. This must be his biggest argument. She turned the page. The passage was circled.

Unfortunately, her Heathcliff was also gone.

And in big, bold red letters, it said:

I AM NOT HEATHCLIFF

Chapter 24

"Annie, are you there? Why is the door locked? Are you okay?" Aaliyah shouted from the front of the house. Annie leaped up, running to let her in. "Oh, thank goodness! I thought I was about to be on the evening news! Author goes missing, mad hunt begins, only witness sexy southerner . . ." Aaliyah continued to mumble as she walked past Annie and looked down at her desk. "Is this the evidence?"

"Yes," Annie said. "But it's really weird. He wrote all these notes, and—"

"Is this as far as you've gotten?" Aaliyah asked, pointing to the big red scribbled *I am not Heathcliff*.

"Yes, and I can't make heads or tails of it. I'm not sure what his claims are, and I don't think 'I am not Heathcliff' is compelling enough to send the police over."

Aaliyah pulled the phone out of her pocket and swiped it. "What time did you say the police were coming?"

"Noon," Annie said.

"Okay, it looks like we have some time." Aaliyah slid the phone back in her pocket. "Here's the plan. I'm going to walk through what you've read and we'll write a rebuttal, then—"

A knock sounded at the door and Annie stared wide-eyed at Aaliyah, the blood draining from her face.

"They're early," Aaliyah whispered. "I was afraid of that. I saw the police car outside when I pulled up."

"Aaliyah!" Annie whimpered, scrutinizing her clothing and tugging at it nervously. "I'm not dressed! I'm still in sweatpants! And I don't understand the evidence enough to refute it, and—"

"It's okay. I've got this." Aaliyah laid her hand on the book. "You answer the door."

"But—"

"Answer the door, and I'll be right there. We'll make it work."

Annie nodded, her hands shaking as she gripped the knob, taking a deep breath as she swung it open. She gave a gasp of relief when she saw Scott there, wearing a suit for court, and not two armed police officers.

"Scott," she breathed. "What is it? I don't have time—"

"I forgot to add my last piece of evidence," he said, holding out a slip of paper that resembled the ones sticking out of the book.

She snatched it, angry that he would waste her precious time. Maybe that was how he planned to win the case; She would be ill prepared in front of the judge. "Anything else?"

"Read it."

She glanced at the strip and read aloud, "'It was easy

enough to win Mrs. Heathcliff's heart. But now, I'm glad you did not try.'" Hurt and frustration raged through Annie. "I don't understand. This is what Nelly says to Mr. Lockwood about Cathy. What does it have to do with anything? How is this evidence?"

"You seem to forget that there are two parts to *Wuthering Heights*, and you spend an obsessive amount of time focusing on the first. Wasn't it you who told me that people often cut out the last part, but it's the most crucial?"

"Of course it's the most crucial! It's the family's second chance not to repeat their parents' mistakes because if Heathcliff and Catherine had just forgiven each other like Cathy and Hareton did, all that awful stuff wouldn't have happened."

"Exactly. Annie, you were right. I'm glad we didn't get married."

"Yeah, well, me too!"

"And I'm not Heathcliff. I'm Hareton."

Annie stopped her rebuttal before she could start it as Scott held out a yellow rose.

"Yellow." She sniffed. "So what? You're offering me friendship now? Are you hoping to settle this peacefully out of court? Because I don't think you have an argument—"

"Annie, why do you never hear what I am trying to say?" Scott snapped. "This is obviously a red-tipped yellow rose, which has nothing to do with friendship."

"What is it, then?" she asked, wondering what riddle

he was trying to frustrate her with now. Were they going to court or not?

"Annie, Catherine Linton couldn't let go of her anger. Neither could Heathcliff. 'Too many times we cling to our pain and refuse to see that life goes on, emotions calm down, and people regret.'"

Annie was surprised to hear her own words quoted back at her.

He shoved the rose forward, and she took it.

"It means to fall in love." He gave a nod of his head and spun around, walking down the path.

Annie's thoughts were racing. Had she missed something? Scott was glad they didn't get married. All his evidence were corrections about how he had really felt. He said he wasn't Heathcliff—he was Hareton, and the difference between the two was . . . She was an idiot.

"Scott," she yelled. He glanced over his shoulder. Her voice was softened as she said, "You answered my love letter."

He stared at her, raising an eyebrow.

"You realize I was right. It wasn't the right time. Heathcliff never forgave. Hareton put the past behind him. Hareton was willing to fall in love with Cathy. Scott, are you saying that, even after all my mistakes, you forgive me?"

He smiled at her, a coy, mischievous smile. "Yes. In return, can you forgive me for my foolish behavior?"

She swallowed, her mouth dry. "Yes," she whispered.

Scott took a step toward her. "Annie, I don't know

you anymore. I don't know what you like, what you've done, or what you want. But I do know that I loved you as much as you loved me. Can we try again?"

Annie couldn't believe what she was hearing. She stared at Scott, his gaze unmoving as he waited for her answer. She took a couple breaths, her nose tingling and throat tightening. Her heart felt like it would burst out of her chest as she made her choice. She ran to Scott, throwing her arms around him and letting out a sob of "yes" into his shoulder. Scott crushed her to him, smelling the fragrance of her hair, the same scent from years before.

"Annie," he breathed.

"Yes?"

"We've waited long enough and I'm not missing any more chances. Can I kiss you now?"

She looked up at him, tears streaming down her face as she nodded. He placed his hands on either side of her face, wiping away the tears with his thumbs as he gazed into her hazel eyes. He traced his finger along her jaw as if he was making sure she was real. Then he smiled, slowly leaning in and accepting a kiss that was willingly given. In that moment, they could feel the past being left behind.

"Aren't you guys the sweetest?"

Annie glanced from Scott's face to look behind her and flushed as she saw Aaliyah standing in the doorway, her phone held up like she was recording.

"What a fairytale ending. I told you I was your fairy

godmother, didn't I?"

Annie's mouth dropped as she put all the pieces together. "You tricked me again!" she cried, moving to approach Aaliyah, but Scott increased his grip, holding her in place. "There is no court date, there are no police, and that lawyer . . . Oh, my goodness, that was my new neighbor. I knew he was familiar, but I was so frazzled, I couldn't place him."

"I gave him the name Mr. Dean, like Nelly Dean, Heathcliff and Catherine's middleman. Do you like that?" Scott asked, rubbing her back to calm her down.

"That is quite poetic," she admitted, then she smacked Scott on the chest. "But you two scared me! I almost called Charles to tell him he was now a full-time dad!"

Aaliyah laughed. "You are so naïve sometimes. You should have trusted your gut, but I'm glad you didn't because what we have here is publicity gold!"

She clicked and swiped on her phone, giggling every few seconds. She must have been posting the video she had taken on the internet.

Annie wasn't sure if she was mad or grateful. Scott laid his hand on her cheek and gently guided her gaze back to him. The aroma that resonated from his suit smelled like his cologne, and she was hit with a wave of nostalgia. She looked into his sapphire eyes, as piercing as they were the first time she saw him, and she felt he knew all her secrets, which, admittedly, he sort of did.

Epilogue

Annie's head rested against Scott's thigh as she napped, her slight frame lying on her side on the wide couch she and Scott had purchased a month after their marriage. Scott absentmindedly stroked her hair while he balanced the laptop on the arm of the couch and edited the photo of his latest family photo shoot. His photography business has taken off since his arrival in Arizona. With such an impressive portfolio, reasonable prices, and charm, he became a local favorite. It didn't hurt that their video had gone viral, endearing the two lovers to the public, especially Arizona, who claimed Annie as their own, though Virginians made a claim for her *and* Scott, seeing as they were raised there and it was the setting for half the novel.

Natalie sat in the corner, lounging in a basket swing Papa Scott had made especially for her so she could sit and write her own books. The living room of their house was large, and the heart of their home. Their paid-off property gave each girl a room of their own with another to spare. For guests, Scott had said. Scott rented out his grandpa's house as an Airbnb with claims that it was the setting for a scene from *He Will Never Know*, and with his savings and Annie's royalties, they found that life could be quite comfortable.

Charles and Melissa were frequent dinner guests, and Annie was often quite surprised at how well the two men got along. Whether it was for the girls' sake or whether they actually grew to like each other, she couldn't tell, but peace resounded through their house and their two families.

Rebecca skipped into the room, smiling widely at Scott. She wrapped her fingers together behind her back as she said in a sing-song voice, "Papa Scott."

"Yes, missy?" he said, immediately shutting his computer and giving her his full attention. "What do you need?"

"Mom gave me a sibling, and you should meet her. Do you know what a sibling is?" she asked.

"I do know. It means a brother or sister. But I already met your sibling. She's right over there."

Natalie smiled, not looking up, but raising her fingers up for a second as if to say, "Hey."

"No, Papa," she said with a giggle. "Not *that* sibling! The one in Mommy's tummy!"

Scott froze, giving a gasp. His eyes immediately fell to his snoozing wife, who was peeking up at him. His gaze shifted to her waist, where she wasn't showing yet.

"Surprise," Annie mumbled.

Scott's heart pounded, his breathing increasing. "Do

you mean it?"

"I know you always wanted kids," she said, pushing herself up. "Now you'll have one."

"Oh, my dear, you are wrong," he said with a shake of his head. "Now I have three."

With that, he pulled Rebecca and Annie into a hug, tickling Rebecca, who giggled and squirmed, kicking her legs out erratically.

"Natalie, save us!" Annie cried, attempting in vain to escape the chaos and laughing at her daughter's delighted giggles. Natalie bounced from her swing and tackled Papa Scott, pulling him to the floor as the two girls turned the tickles on him.

"No, no! I give up!" he cried. The girls stopped, still watching him warily. "Just kidding! I will never admit defeat!"

Screams and laughter filled the house as the group wrestled together, tickling and hugging and running away only to return for another try.

The battle only stopped because a knock came from the front door.

"Daddy!" Rebecca screamed.

"I'll get it!" Natalie yelled.

Both girls sprang to their feet, scrambling over each other to be the first to get to the door. Annie chuckled as Scott rose, and they both entered the kitchen in time to greet Charles and Melissa.

"How was the drive?" Annie asked Melissa as she gave her a hug.

"Not too bad," she replied. "I brought over some rolls to go with the roast and some extra apples for the girls. I hope that's okay."

"Oh, wonderful!" Annie said. "The roast should be done any minute, and I have some mashed potatoes to go with it. You didn't happen to bring over some of your cinnamon honey butter, did you?"

Melissa smiled as she pulled out a square container. "I did."

Annie clapped excitedly.

"Good. I'm starving," Charles said with a grin. "And this sounds like the perfect meal."

"Daddy," Rebecca said, tugging on his sleeve. "Mommy's going to have a baby."

Charles glanced between Scott and Annie, his face going from surprise to smiling. "Really?"

Annie sighed. "We were going to keep it a secret a little longer."

"I'm so happy for you," he said, giving Annie a hug. "Congratulations, Scott." He gave Scott a hearty handshake.

"I only just found out myself," Scott admitted.

"Still in shock, then?" Charles said with a laugh.

"Yeah." Scott chuckled. "Pretty much."

Melissa and Annie finished prepping the food while the rest of the family banded together to get the table set and ready for dinner. When they all sat down and after prayer, plate-filling, and the quiet that comes with the beginning of a meal, Scott asked, "What do you think we should name the baby?"

"I know exactly what we're naming it," Annie said.

"Don't I get a say?" Scott replied.

"No."

"Be careful, Scott. You don't want to know the names she picked out for the girls before I vetoed them," Charles said.

"Celestia Galatea is a perfectly good name!" Annie snapped.

"I could have been Celestia Galatea?" Natalie cried. "That's an epic name! There's another Natalie in my class, and I have to go by Allred so it's not confusing."

"Blame your father," Annie said. "I wanted cool names."

"I wasn't nervous before," Scott said. "But now…"

Annie rolled her eyes. "They are perfectly normal names."

Charles and Melissa chuckled as Scott took a deep breath. "Okay. Let's hear them."

Annie waited a moment, enjoying everyone's looks of anticipation. "If it's a girl . . . Catherine."

"That's lovely," Melissa said.

Scott sighed, grinning. "And if it's a boy?"

Annie's eyes sparkled at Scott as she said, "Hareton."

Charles snorted, pretending to cough into his napkin.

"That's unique," Melissa said encouragingly while she thumped Charles on the back harder than necessary.

Scott scoffed. "We're not naming him Hareton."

"Why not?" Annie asked.

"Because that's a weird name. No one names their

kid Hareton."

"That's why it's perfect. A unique kid from a unique situation," Annie argued.

"No, that's not happening."

She sat up straighter and looked him in the eye. "I can name my kid whatever I want. I'm an author. It's acceptable and supposed to be weird and cliché. We have a very public story, and this makes the book ending sweet and encourages the reader to say 'Aww.'"

Scott shook his head. "No, I don't care. You can name your book kids whatever you like, but we are not naming any son of mine Hareton!"

When Hareton Scott was born and his father held the tiny baby in his arms for the first time, he beamed over at his wife and realized he had gotten everything he'd wanted out of life. Because of a romance novel, Annie got her second chance. And so did he.

Thank you for reading *He Will Never Know*. Please leave a review on Amazon, Goodreads, and anywhere else possible. Reviews help your favorite authors continue to write!

I would love to connect to you!
facebook.com/authortoneylarson

Acknowledgements

I'd like to take this time to say thank you to my husband, who has put up with my writing shenanigans for a long, long time. Thank you to Tristi Pinkston, an amazing writer and editor who helped polish this work. Thank you to Jenni James for encouraging me and inspiring me to write (and to branch out into romance!). And thank you to my MOMMs (Ministering Moms of Multiples). These amazing mamas beta read, critiqued, and picked the cover designs for your reading and viewing pleasure. And they did it all while wrangling multiples. You are super women and deserve a break. I hope this book gives you a little one. (If you know any moms of multiples, help them out. They are not ok.)

About the Author

When Toney Larson was a child, she dreamed of being a writer. When she grew up, she acted more responsibly and went to art school. After graduating with a B.A. in fine art, she continued her education and earned a B.S. and MBA. Toney reworked the Rapunzel fairytale in her first book, *Growing Amaranth*. Since then, she has continued to add tales to her YA fantasy series *Legends of Draven,* as well as branch out into non-fiction and Romance. *He Will Never Know* was written in five days after a dream and a minor bout of insanity. A current resident of Utah, Toney lives with her grizzly bear husband and six remarkable (and too good to her) children. When she's not writing she spends her time in graphic design, homeschooling, and homesteading.

Made in the USA
Middletown, DE
17 March 2022